An Instructive Mountie

Adventures of the First Woman Mountie. Book 12

LAURIE SCHRAMM

Print ISBN: 978-1-7387599-6-5
ePub ISBN: 978-1-7387599-7-2

Laurie Schramm

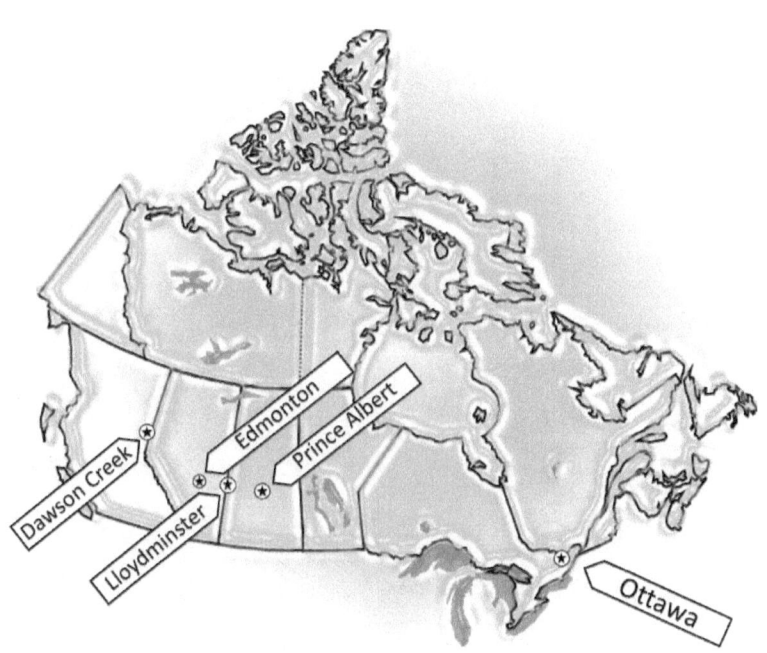

Laurie Schramm

DEDICATION

To Dr. Alexander (Sandy) Beveridge, Ph.D., FCIC (1940 – 2014), a forensic chemist who spent 30 years in the Forensic Science Service of the RCMP. Among his areas of expertise were the chemistry of explosives and explosive residues, for which he was internationally recognized.

and

To Kent who, for a time, was a forensic document examiner in the Forensic Science Service of the RCMP before he moved on to serve Canada in another capacity.

.

Laurie Schramm

CONTENTS

Laurie Schramm

ACKNOWLEDGMENTS

I am extremely grateful to the growing number of friendly readers that that have provided encouragement, comments, and suggestions based on drafts of these books: Ann Marie, Katherine, Victoria, William, Dawson, Al, Jayme, Karen M., and Ernie.

Special thanks also to three real-life veterans of the RCMP, all of whom have supplemented their encouragement with background, advice, and factual reference materials on the Force: Chief Superintendent William Schramm (Ret.), who also kindly allowed my main character to borrow his Regimental Number, Assistant Commissioner Dawson Hovey (Ret.), Deputy Commissioner Peter German, KC, Ph.D. (Ret.), Constable Karen Frost (Ret., one of the trailblazing women Mounties who joined-up when women represented only 2% of the total uniformed complement), and especially Staff Sergeant Al Lund (Ret., author of *Mounties on the Cover* and probably the world's leading authority on Mountie fiction).

Laurie Schramm

LIST OF CHARACTERS
(IN ORDER OF APPEARANCE)

- Frank Smith (not his real name), an escaped prisoner
- Corporal Alexandra (Alex) Houston, RCMP Security Service
- Silver, an Alaskan Malamute; and Alex's friend and police-service-dog partner
- Staff Sergeant Robert (Bob) Simpson, RCMP Security Service
- Dr. Barry McDecy, Ph.D., RCMP Forensic Science Service
- Gerald (Gerry) Tate, RCMP Forensic Science Service
- Staff Sergeant William (Bill) Preston, RCMP Dog Service
- Constable Julie Sawyer, RCMP Dog Service
- Scout, a German Shepherd; and Julie's friend and police-service-dog partner
- Edward (Ed) Williams, Chief of Security, Trans-Mountain
- Captain Donald (Don) Harrison, Military Intelligence, Canadian Armed Forces

LIST OF ACRONYMS AND ABBREVIATIONS

CPIC   Canadian Police Information Centre
FCIC   Fellow of the Chemical Institute of Canada
HQ   Headquarters
NRCan   Natural Resources Canada
OPP   Ontario Provincial Police
PDS   Police Dog Service
PSD   Police Service Dog
RCMP   Royal Canadian Mounted Police
UHF   Ultra-High Frequency

1 THE SEEDS OF DESTRUCTION

August 6, 1979
Prince Albert, Saskatchewan

It was a dreary day in Northern Saskatchewan. Summer would soon give way to fall and this seemed like a symbol of the coming change: it was cool and overcast with heavy clouds, and a light rain was beginning to fall. Not, in short, the kind of day that most people would rush out and embrace with an enthusiastic smile, but the kind that leave most people wanting to simply stay home in bed or, failing that, to resignedly trudge out and attempt to get it over with. It was clearly the latter attitude that had been adopted by the three, rather forlorn-looking, men who slowly walked out of the Saskatchewan Federal Penitentiary, near Prince Albert, and climbed into a plain, unmarked prison van. The attitude of the two guards could, perhaps, be explained by the weather, but their prisoner would normally have appeared to be in good cheer. Such cheeriness would surprise anyone who knew him well, but then no one in the prison knew him well.

Four years earlier, in 1975, he'd been convicted of murder and sent to the Saskatchewan Federal Penitentiary and incarcerated in its high-security area. Two years later, good conduct, a perpetual outward-appearance of cheerfulness, and a carefully cultivated, friendly relationship with the prison staff distinguished him from the majority of the inmates who tended to be morose and withdrawn, and certainly from the roughly one-third of the

1

inmates, who tended to be angry, surly, and prone to violence. The prison, like so many others, was not well funded and had evolved over time to rely quite heavily on the unpaid work of trusted prisoners who were willing to work as a way to pass the time and add some diversity to an otherwise dull routine. These trusties, as they were called, were allowed – encouraged even – to perform janitorial, clerical, warehousing, cooking, cleaning, and other tasks for which they were given extra freedom and privileges in lieu of pay. In this prisoner's case, he had gravitated to the prison workshop, where his obvious skill with tools led to him teaching other inmates and eventually becoming the workshop supervisor. In this position, it was easy for him to construct a slender, easily concealed knife and several kinds of lock-picking tools, all of which he concealed in a hidden compartment of a leather belt that he had also made for himself.

Now, on this dreary day, he had dropped his cheerful and friendly guise in favour of a dudgeon combined with an air of pain and discomfort. This wasn't very difficult because his inner nature was to be rather sullen and discontent, and he really was in some pain due to the ear infection that had been diagnosed by the resident nurse at the prison infirmary. So it was, that the prisoner and his two guards clambered into the prison van and drove to the Holy Family Hospital[1] in Prince Albert to get his ear infection treated.

After being given an antibiotic by one of the physicians, the prisoner said he had to use the toilet and, was allowed to go into the men's washroom unsupervised, although he still wore leg-irons and the guards had agreed to unlock one side of his handcuffs. Being on the third floor, the guards probably judged that it was too high up for him to jump out the window and, in any case, he was a trustie after all, and he was still confined with the leg-irons.

Once he was in the washroom and out of the guard's sight, the prisoner picked the locks on his handcuffs and leg-irons, tossed them in a garbage bin, and promptly crawled out one of the windows. From there, he was able to make his way along a narrow ledge and re-enter the hospital through the open window of an unoccupied recovery room. Cautiously walking towards the door leading to an operating theatre, he could hear the indistinct sounds of several voices. Creeping closer, and placing an ear to one door, he was able to hear enough to judge that an operation was underway.

Perfect, he thought, *that should keep them busy.*

Searching around, he found a laundry hamper in one corner of the room, from which he was able to select a set of hospital scrubs that fit him reasonably well and didn't appear to be overly soiled. Replacing his prison uniform with the scrubs, and placing his prison garb at the bottom of the hamper, all that remained was to watch for the hallway to become busy, and then calmly walk out and away from the direction of the guards, who were just then entering the washroom to check on him.

As the guards, having found the washroom to be empty of their prisoner, rushed back out to the corridor to begin a frantic search, he was already out of their line of sight, walking down one of the staircases that led to the rear of the hospital. Continuing all the way to the basement, he located the morgue and entered the pathologists' locker and shower room. Several of the steel lockers appeared to be in use, as they had padlocks on them, and he was relieved to note that the lockers were of the same design as his old high-school lockers had been. In other words, the doors were secured by hinged vertical bars that projected into holes at the top and bottom of the doorframe, and which were moved by the lifting of a latch once its padlock had been removed. What he had learned as a high-school student was that such doors could easily be opened by inserting a steel ruler into the gap between the door and frame and, with one tip of the ruler jammed against the lower of the vertical bars, the mechanism could be independently actuated, opening the door. He didn't have a steel ruler anymore, but he did have a knife.

The first locker he tried was empty. The second had clothes that were too large for him, but an adjustable baseball cap, so he extracted the latter. The third locker he tried yielded a bonanza: a serviceable set of acceptably fitting street clothes, a wallet identifying its owner as a physician, and a set of car and house keys. which he simply carried out with him. A brief period in another washroom down the hall enabled him to change out of the scrubs and into the newly stolen clothes, after which he emerged into the corridor once again and then calmly walked back upstairs to the main floor and out one of the rear doorways.

The prison guards, meanwhile, had conducted a quick but fruitless search of the third floor, called in to report the prisoner's escape, and were moving to take up positions at the main front and rear doors to keep watch while they waited for reinforcements. The guard that ran to the back door actually saw the prisoner walking towards one of the parking lots but didn't recognise him. The guard was looking for someone in a prison uniform, not regular street clothes and a cap.

As the prison guard went back into the hospital to continue searching, the prisoner headed for the staff parking lot and began checking the most expensive-looking vehicles, looking for that belonging to the physician whose wallet, keys, and clothes he'd stolen. The keys were for a Volvo, and the only one in sight was a fairly new-looking station wagon. That was the one. Settling himself in the car, he backed out and drove away, heading south to Saskatoon.

As he did so, he kept an eye out for roadside towns that were small – small enough to have no bank, and therefore no automatic cash dispenser. At such small towns, he knew, any local residents needing extra cash would go to the local gas station to buy a few small items and ask the attendant to put a larger amount on their credit card, taking the difference as cash. At the first such stop he checked the physician's wallet more carefully. It contained nearly two hundred dollars in cash[2] and two credit cards. Using one of the credit cards, he bought a few things and asked for an extra forty dollars in cash. He repeated this at several small towns along the way, alternating credit cards and being careful not to ask for too much cash at any one store. The prisoner was fully aware that his actions would create a trail for the police, but he wasn't very concerned. He had a plan for that.

When he reached Saskatoon, the prisoner alternated using the two credit cards to buy some additional clothes and a suitcase at a second-hand store, then bought a large stock of mostly non-perishable food and drinks at a grocery store, then a large gasoline can and some tools at a hardware store, then filled the gasoline can and the Volvo's tank at a gas station. When he went to a liquor store, he discovered he'd reached the credit limit on one of the cards, so he switched to the second. With the Volvo thus loaded, he drove to the Yellowhead Highway heading west towards the Alberta border,

The next question was how long it would be before the physician noticed that his clothes and wallet (and car) were gone and whether he would first call the police or the credit card companies. He'd escaped from the hospital at about 9:30 am, and estimated that the theft would be discovered no later than about 11:30. He guessed that the police would be called first, and the credit card companies second, and figured that might buy him an additional 30 minutes. Accordingly, he made two more small town stops to get more cash from the second credit card then threw them both away.

When he reached Lloydminster, which straddled the Alberta/Saskatchewan border, he went looking for a large industrial plant of some kind and ended up at a large oil refinery on the Alberta side, in the city's northwest corner. At the refinery, he drove into the middle of the large employee parking lot, which was quite full, and found an empty parking space. Pulling into it, he reached for a flat-bladed screwdriver, got out of the car, and casually walked to the front of the vehicle parked beside him. There he knelt down and unscrewed the front licence plate[3]. Moving nonchalantly to the vehicle on the other side of his stolen Volvo, he removed its front licence plate as well. Walking to the back of this, second vehicle, he knelt down and replaced the rear plate – the one with the 1979 registration sticker on it - with the plain one that had been on the front of the first vehicle. He then had the front and rear plates from the second vehicle, while leaving both vehicles with rear plates but no front plates. He knew that the vehicles' owners would identify their respective vehicles by their make, model, and colour, and he figured - correctly, as it turned out - that it would be many days before either owner noticed that anything was amiss with their licence plates. In fact, the second driver was only alerted when he was stopped by the police two weeks later in a routine traffic stop. He was naturally unable to explain to the police why he had no front licence plate, nor why his rear plate had no registration renewal sticker on it and did not match the number on his registration certificate. The owner of the first vehicle only became aware of the problem when she was contacted by the police, who had checked on the second vehicle's plate number for its rightful owner.

The next stop was to check-in at an older-type motel on one edge of the city that had seen better days but which, judging by the nearly full parking lot of pickup trucks, seemed to be getting a lot of business from the oilfield service crews. At the motel, he obtained a room for a single night, for which he paid the full bill in advance, in cash. Before leaving, he transferred everything he had purchased from the Volvo to his motel room.

Next, he drove around looking to find used-car dealers of the kind that dealt in vehicles of somewhat questionable driving history and condition, and that would be used to making cash deals. In this he didn't have much trouble, as there were several to choose from and, in fact, he chose two. At the first one, he negotiated the sale of the Volvo, producing the physician's driver's licence and vehicle registration certificate, and explaining that he'd been gambling heavily, had a run of bad luck, and needed to quickly pay off his debts to the kind of people that only accepted cash. The dealer, who had heard hard luck stories of all kinds, either accepted his story or (more likely) didn't care, glanced at the paper work, looked over the Volvo, and then offered the prisoner a low price, probably about a quarter of its market value, the prisoner estimated. After protracted dickering back and forth, they eventually settled on an amount the prisoner estimated to be about two-thirds of its market value. Once he'd collected his money and handed over the keys, he telephoned for a taxi, which he directed to take him to the second used-car lot he'd chosen.

At this second car lot, he looked everything over very carefully for something that would match his two priorities: good mechanical condition and something that looked nothing like a Volvo station wagon. His ultimate selection was an older-model pickup truck for which he negotiated a reasonable price that was far less than he'd just received for the Volvo, and paid for it in cash. When asked to provide a name and address, he made up both on the spot. He decided that he would be Frank Smith, and he provided legitimate-sounding address and phone number in the city (having made a note of the number of the phone he'd used in the previous car-lot). When the salesman handed over the truck's keys, he got in and drove it away, saying that he'd take the risk of driving it, un-plated, to the nearest vehicle registration office. This was such a common practice that the salesman didn't even raise an eyebrow.

When he was a few blocks away from the second used-car lot, the freshly renamed Frank Smith pulled into a convenient parking lot and installed the matching set of Alberta licence plates that he'd brought with him. His next stop was a large hardware store, at which he purchased some plastic sheeting, painter's masking tape, and a number of cans of aerosol spray paint in a flat, forest green colour. The rest of his afternoon was spent behind an old, abandoned warehouse-type building on the outskirts of the city where the truck was sheltered from the wind and largely away from public sight. After removing and discarding the hub caps then masking the windows and lights with the plastic sheeting and masking tape, he used one can after another to paint everything else but the tires in the 'military' green, even the wheels and chrome bumpers. When he was done and had removed the tape and sheeting, the truck actually looked very much like an army truck.

The next day, Frank Smith enjoyed a hearty traveller's breakfast, loaded up his green truck, and headed for the Yellowhead Highway again. This time, however, he headed east. Knowing full well that the police would be looking for an escaped prisoner driving west in a late model Volvo station-wagon bearing Saskatchewan plates, he would be an ordinary citizen driving east in an army-surplus pickup truck bearing Alberta plates. Of course, he still had no valid identification, nor proper vehicle registration or insurance, so he planned to drive carefully and trust to luck that he wouldn't be stopped by the police. Now that he was out of prison, there were some things he needed to do.

As it turned out, Frank Smith was lucky; he made it all the way to Northern Ontario without incident.

The Daily News

Monday, August 6, 1979

Escaped Murderer Loose
Guards' Negligence Blamed

Laurie Schramm

Saturday, November 10, 1979
Near Ottawa, Ontario

Just west of Ottawa (but before Arnprior), and slightly south of
the Ottawa River, Frank Smith was crouched low beside a set of
train tracks, right at the point where the tracks began to cross a
small bridge. He was busy placing a bomb beside one of the rails.

This was no ordinary bomb. He had spent several years, while
incarcerated in the Saskatchewan Federal Penitentiary at Prince
Albert, studying the art of bomb-making from a fellow inmate that
had been willing to teach him in return for lessons in wood- and
metalworking. Then, following his escape from prison, he had
established himself in an isolated cabin in Northern Ontario
experimenting with different formulations and testing them in an
abandoned quarry. Ultimately, he had come up with a nitrate-type,
binary explosive of his own design. Nitrate meant that it was based
on a chemical reaction between ammonium nitrate and ammonium
perchlorate. Binary meant that the explosive comprised two parts,
each in a separate bottle such that neither bottle was explosive on
its own – it was only dangerous after the contents were mixed
together. This meant that it was safe to carry – both in terms of
explosion risk and also legal risk, because it wasn't technically an
explosive until the two parts were mixed together. If he was caught
carrying the two bottles, he planned to claim that they were parts of
an exploding target he had made for the purpose of target practise
at an approved gun range – all very legal[4]. Of course, he planned to
use the explosive in a very illegal way, beginning with the particular
piece of track beside which he was crouched.

From his backpack, he withdrew two plastic bottles. The larger
bottle contained a mixture of two powerful oxidizers, ammonium
nitrate and one other, each having been individually ground to
specific particle sizes and then mixed together in a very specific
ratio[5] in order to achieve an extremely high detonation-success rate
and a powerful blast. The second, smaller bottle contained an
explosive-grade metal powder mixed with small amounts of several
other metal powders, all of the powders also having been
individually ground to specific particle sizes and then mixed
together in very specific, but different ratios from those in the first
bottle. Taking the second bottle, he carefully poured the entire
contents into the first bottle, replaced the cap on the latter and

8

then shook the bottle to produce a reasonably uniform mixture of all of the various components.

He gazed at the first bottle. It hadn't been a bomb before, but it was now. Even so, a feature of this particular kind of bomb was that it was still reasonably safe: it wasn't flammable and couldn't be detonated by friction. Detonation would require the high-impulse energy of a centre-fire rifle round[6], such as from a .308-calibre hunting rifle, which was precisely the kind of rifle he had in his truck.

Next, he withdrew from his backpack, a third bottle. This one was full of gasoline. Using a small trowel, he dug away some of the gravel underneath the rail, between two of the big wooden ties. Into this space, he wedged the two bottles. The wide screw cap on the bottle containing the bomb had been painted a very bright, fluorescent orange. Stepping back from the tracks, he verified that the orange cap was clearly visible. Given the thin layer of fresh, white snow on the ground it stood out very clearly indeed.

Finally, Frank picked up his pack and walked across the short gully over which the bridge passed, and repeated his actions, placing a second bomb where the tracks left the bridge and reconnected with the ground. He now had one bomb placed at each end of the bridge.

Satisfied, Frank hiked back to the place he had parked his truck, which was about a quarter of a mile away and behind a small hill, out of sight of the rail line.

When he reached the truck, Frank traded his backpack for a .308-calibre Winchester hunting rifle, an old tarp, and a white bedsheet. Slinging the rifle over his shoulder, and carrying the rest, he walked to the crest of the nearby hill, spread the tarp out on the snow and took up a prone position where he had a good view of the rail line and the place where it crossed the small bridge. The white sheet he draped over his body and the tarp, so that only his face, arms and rifle were exposed. From inside his jacket, he withdrew a white toque, which he donned.

Time to settle in to wait, he thought. Even with the tarp, it was cold lying on the snow, and the dampness in the air made it feel even colder than the dry prairie cold he was used to, but he used the cold to help him stay focused. He had estimated that a particular freight train would reach the bridge in about another 30 minutes and, sure enough, when half an hour had passed, he could hear a train horn in the distance, and shortly after that, the sounds of an approaching train.

The approaching freight train comprised three locomotives, over a hundred freight cars, and a caboose. Among the cars carrying dangerous goods was a series of tankers filled with propane. Some of the other tankers and boxcars carried a variety of other highly flammable materials. The train carried a crew of four, with two in the lead locomotive and two in the caboose at the rear. As the train rolled along at about 70 kilometres per hour, the engineer and the head-end brakeman in the front locomotive were casually chatting about everything and nothing as they kept a casual lookout ahead for the usual railway signs and signals. Similarly, the conductor and the tail-end brakeman in the caboose[7] were sitting high up in the cupola (the raised section on the roof of the caboose), from which vantage point they could look down the length of the train. They, too, were chatting casually as they kept an eye out for anything out of the ordinary on the train ahead.

As the train came into sight, Frank peered intently through his rifle's telescopic sight and he slightly increased the pressure of his trigger finger on the trigger. Had the engineer, who sat on the right-hand side of the locomotive, chanced to look over at the top of the hill, it's unlikely he would have been able see anything unusual. In addition to the distance involved, very little of Frank's upper body was exposed. He wore a white cap, and had covered his hearing protectors with white adhesive tape so his head would blend-in with the snow. Frank allowed the three locomotives and all of the leading boxcars to pass over the bridge, but when the first of the tankers approached, he squeezed the trigger. He didn't know which of the tankers carried the most flammable materials but, for his purposes, it didn't really matter.

Several things happened then, in rapid succession.

Frank's shoulder recoiled from the force of the shot which sounded something like the crack of a whip and was loud: at nearly 170 dB, it was louder than being near a fighter jet taking off.

The train crew heard the shot.

"What the hell was that?" said the engineer, who was the next closest to Frank's position.

"I think something just blew," said tail-end brakeman in the caboose. "Better signal the guys up front."

"Right," said the conductor, pulling on the emergency brake.

Simultaneously, all the crew members got their answer. There was a loud explosion as the binary explosive detonated and ignited the can of gasoline. The explosive alone would have done the job, but with the added power from the gasoline, the tanker rolling over it had no chance. As that particular tanker was carrying propane, it immediately exploded into a huge orange fireball that rose up 300 metres.

"Look at that!" said the head-end brakeman to the engineer. "One of the tankers has gone up." He instinctively reached for the brakes, but the engineer's words stopped him.

"No! Not the brakes. We need to pull what cars we can away from that explosion." Adding power, he kept the front end of the train moving forward.

Meanwhile, the cars behind the exploding tanker still had momentum propelling them and with a wave of screeching, tearing, and banging, the following tankers in the train began to smash into each other, causing some to crush, some to jack-knife upwards, and others to tip over and off of the rails.

As Frank watched from his vantage point on the hill, his jaw dropped at the drama unfolding in front of him: more explosions, more sounds of smashing and tearing metal, a set of train wheels spinning into the air, one entire tanker being lifted high into the air before itself exploding into another fireball and then raining fire down to the ground.

From the cupola of their caboose, the conductor and the tail-end brakeman had a similar view, and watched, frozen for a moment in horror. Then, shaking himself back into alertness, the conductor reached for his radio-telephone to call in an alarm. He'd no sooner transmitted the alert than the caboose smashed into the wreckage in front of them. As the caboose was twisted up and off the rails, the entire cupola was ripped away, carrying its human cargo with it.

Given the number of cars carrying dangerous goods on the train, all available police and fire personnel in the area were called to respond[8].

2 THE FIRST CALL

"E007, 10-21," the radio in my truck crackled to life.

My name is Corporal Alexandra Houston, Royal Canadian Mounted Police (RCMP) Security Service. My friends call me Alex. E007 was the call-sign assigned to my radio. The letter E designated my unit as operational support. This prefix was assigned to unmarked police-dog-service (PDS) or forensic (IDENT) units, in my case I'm also a dog master and I always travel with Silver, an Alaskan Malamute, my friend and partner. The number '007' showed that my boss, Staff Sergeant Robert (Bob) Simpson, had a sense of humour (he often jokes that I'm like some kind of female James Bond). As if my Security Service posting didn't give me enough variety, we were often called out in our capacity as a PDS team. In fact, on this chilly Saturday in November, we were just then returning from being called out to help with a search for a lost child.

"E007," I acknowledged.

"What's your twenty?" By 'twenty' the radio-room dispatcher meant 10-20, the code for location.

"East side, travelling west on the Queensway." This was in Ottawa, Ontario, where I'm normally based.

"We have a request from the OPP[9] for all available units to respond to a major freight train derailment at the Galetta Railway Bridge, near Arnprior. They've specifically requested a PDS team.

Can you respond."

"E007, 10-4," I responded meaning that I was acknowledging receipt of the message and that I would handle it 'as requested.'

"Continue west on Highway 417, then take the Galetta Side Road to Galetta, where a check-point has been established. OPP says 10-18, and requests Code 3." 10-18 meant urgent, and Code 3 meant proceed over the speed limit, with lights and siren.

"E007, 10-17," I responded meaning that I was enroute.

"Another call," I remarked to Silver as I signalled and pulled over to the side of the road so I could reach into the glove compartment for my magnetic-base, flashing red light. Rolling down my side window, I tossed it up and over so it would land on the roof and then plugged the cord into the truck's cigarette-lighter socket. Over the years, I had become quite good at tossing the light up and onto the roof. Then I switched on my signal lights and siren and, after checking my rear-view mirrors and a quick glance into my blind-spot, I re-entered the freeway traffic and accelerated into the passing lane.

In just over half an hour, we were slowing down to enter the town of Galetta and I could already see the red flashing lights of the checkpoint that had been set up. From the checkpoint we were directed southeast, taking us a few kilometres outside of town to where a rail line crossed the ice-covered Mississippi River[10]. I say directed, but in fact we were simply waved into a convey of emergency vehicles that were all headed to the same place: marked police cars from several police services, fire trucks, ambulances, and even a mobile command centre.

As soon as we left the town I could see why: a huge red glow illuminated the two steel trusses of the bridge.

When we reached the scene, I radioed "E007, 10-23," to let the RCMP room know we'd arrived 'on scene.' There was an OPP sergeant directing traffic and we were waved to one of several staging areas where another sergeant asked us to help search for two of the train's crewmembers that had been in the disabled caboose and were now missing. For this, we were partnered with an OPP Constable that had a portable, handheld UHF radio that was set to the local command centre's main channel. They also gave me a heavy shirt and a jacket, not the same size, that had been recovered from the wrecked caboose and were thought to belong to the two missing crew members.

I had initially thought that the burning rail cars I'd glimpsed were just a big fire, but I had to quickly revise that notion when there was a thundering blast as a propane tanker exploded into a bright orange fireball, followed by a wave of heat that reached all the way back to where we were standing.

"Be careful out there," said the sergeant.

"Riightt," I replied, thoughtfully. It occurred to me that the way to 'be careful' would be to get back into the truck and go home, but I didn't say so. We'd been called in to do a job, so on we went.

When we came upon the caboose, it was lying on its side and tangled up with two flat cars that had originally been carrying loads of steel pipe. The cupola that had been sheared off the caboose lay about ten metres north of that, so we decided to search a series of concentric arcs beginning at the remains of the caboose and radiating northward to the cupola and beyond. Meanwhile, I had given Silver the two recovered garments to sniff and set him on a long lead to try to pick the scents.

Although we had to tramp around in the snow, it did make it easier to spot foreign objects. It was tedious though. Search and arc, turn, search an arc, turn, and so on. After quite a few such arcs, we began to find things: the conductor's cap in one spot, a coffee cup in another.... Several switchbacks later, Silver began to find splotches of blood, and then a body which, by its clothing we took to be that of the rear brakeman.

Whatever had sheared the cupola off the caboose apparently had caught the brakeman at the same time and sheared away one arm and part of his shoulder. At some point he had been either torn-out or ejected from the caboose. I hoped that he'd died quickly, at least, without suffering.

The constable agreed to go back for a body bag while Silver and I continued to search for the conductor, and he offered to loan me his portable radio in case I found anything or got into trouble. Several switchbacks later, Silver caught another scent and struck off determinedly to one side. A few moments later he suddenly sat down on his haunches and looked back at me. Due to the noise from the ongoing fires and firefighting efforts it was quite noisy, so I couldn't hear the moaning sounds until I was crouching down over the sprawled figure that Silver had found.

"Good boy Silver!" I congratulated. "What'd you find?"

It was the conductor, and he was breathing! I imagined that he mustn't have been wearing a seatbelt when the crash occurred, and that he'd simply been ejected from the caboose. When the cupola was sheared off, he was fortunate not to have been torn-up at the same time.

Breathing was good, but his pulse was weak and something about the position of the conductor's body made me worry about the possibility of neck or spinal injury so I decided that, as long as he continued breathing, I wouldn't try to move him. Using the constable's radio, I was able to contact the sergeant at the marshalling point from which we'd set out, explain what I'd found, and ask for paramedics and a spinal board.

Since ambulances had begun arriving at about the time I did, there were paramedics close at hand and it wasn't long before I heard the voice of the constable calling out for me.

Once they'd arrived and looked things over, the paramedics decided they were concerned about the conductor's neck and spine too and, under their direction, the constable and I helped them to very carefully stretch-out the conductor's body and place it on the spinal board where they could secure him for transport. With that done, all four of us took up position at the corners and carefully walked the patient out of the crash zone and over to a waiting ambulance. As they left for the nearest hospital, the sergeant at our marshalling point assigned the constable to traffic duty somewhere further along the derailment site and thanked me (and Silver) for coming out to help.

"You're welcome," I replied. "Searching for people isn't Silver's primary training so we don't get as much practice as I'd like, and I'm always relieved when we have a successful search.

"Really?" said the sergeant, "what's his primary training then?"

"Explosives."

The sergeant just looked at me for a moment, then shook himself and said, "Would you mind waiting around for a moment while I talk to someone?"

"No, we can hang around," I said. My face must have indicated the obvious question that was on my mind, but the sergeant had already walked over to his cruiser to call someone on his radio. As I watched, I could track his attempt to reach someone, get a connection, then have a brief but animated conversation, after which he waved me over to his car.

"One of our people has found something that looks suspicious. Apparently, it doesn't look like a bomb, but it looks out of place and the constable that found it had the presence of mind to leave it alone and report it to his supervisor. They're both coming here now. Would you be willing to go with them and take a look for us?"

"Sure," I replied. "If it's OK with you, Silver and I will just go warm up in my truck over there."

We were just getting the chill out of our bodies when an OPP highway patrol car rolled up and a sergeant and constable got out and come over. Once introductions were complete, the sergeant told his constable to tell me what she'd found.

"Well, I was on the other side of the wreck walking back from the locomotives towards the bridge when I noticed something strange: it was circular, international orange, and about three-and-a-half inches in diameter. It really stood out against the snow, so I walked over to see what it was. It seems to be the screw-on cap of a large bottle, maybe a quart or a quart -and-a-half, and it was lying right beside another bottle of about the same size, but with a regular cap. The things is, the bottles had been shoved into a space someone had dug out under a rail and between two ties, and it's right where the bridge deck meets up with the shore on the far side of the river.

"I was just about to try to dig it out when a little alarm bell went off in my head and I realized it might be a bomb."

"What's your first name constable?" I asked.

"Emily."

"Well Emily, I think you played it smart. I'm not an explosives expert, but let's go take a look and we'll see what Silver's nose tells him."

So, they went back to their car and Silver and I followed them in my truck. It took a few minutes because we had to drive away from the crash scene, back the way I had originally come in, then take a cross-road and then another, in order to get around the area where the firefighters were still trying to suppress the burning rail cars, and then drive in as close as possible to the front of the train. Then, we all got out and walked, along the north side of the tracks, beside the three locomotives and the unaffected rail cars before we finally came to the first of the two trusses that supported the train bridge.

When we were about five metres from the edge of the bridge Emily stopped and pointed. Sure enough, there was a bright orange disc exactly where she had said it would be.

I gave Silver the command and hand signal associated with 'search for explosives' and set him out on my long lead. He did his usual sniffing around that always began looking like a 'random walk' to me but seemed to make some kind of sense to him, and then the span of his search narrowed and narrowed until he ended up right beside the orange disk, at which point he sat down on his haunches and looked directly at me.

"Looks like Silver agrees with you," I said, and the three of us walked up for a closer look.

After we'd all looked, but not touched, I said to the sergeant "I think Emily has found a bomb, but the derailment happened over at the far end of the bridge." I raised one eyebrow quizzically.

He took the cue. "You think there was a second bomb over there? One that did go off?"

"It's only a guess, but it's stretching the odds to think that the train would have accidentally derailed so close to the point where someone went to all the trouble of placing a bomb."

"I agree," he said. "I'll call for the bomb squad[11] and ask that they look at both locations."

The next afternoon, Silver and I went to visit the conductor. He had regained consciousness overnight and the hospital was apparently holding him for observation. From his hospital bed he vividly described how terrifying it had been when the rail cars ahead of him had begun to derail, pile into one another, and/or fly off the tracks.

"Before I could even react," he continued, "the car in front of us tipped upwards at the back and Fred, the tail-end brakeman, and I saw the rear end coming straight at us in the cupola! I felt myself flying through the air, and then hitting something. The next thing I knew, I was lying in a hospital bed.

"There was an OPP constable in to see me this morning," he concluded, "and he told me about Fred, and that it was you two that found me lying in the snow, unconscious, and got help. I sure owe you my life!"

I told him that we'd found Fred and that I thought he probably died instantly and without suffering. As far as saving him, I said it was our pleasure, that I was just glad Silver had been able to find him in time, and that I wished him a speedy recovery.

As Silver and I left, I felt mixed emotions: sadness for the dead brakeman, happiness for the recovering conductor, and pleasure in Silver's ability to find him.

When I was back in the office after the week-end, I gave my boss a summary of our activities at the site of the train derailment, concluding with my recommendation that the OPP have bomb experts look at the locations of the initial derailment point and the suspicious package that had been found.

"The OPP sergeant on the scene agreed to call in their bomb squad, but I think it would be good to have one of our forensic-explosives experts from Identification Services[12] go look at the device before the bomb squad blows it up. It looked like something new to me, and I think it might be helpful to know how it was made."

"I agree," said Bob. "I'll make a few calls."

A week after the derailment, I received a request to meet with the Force's principal forensics expert in explosives at Identification Services - Ottawa, which housed one of the Force's several forensic laboratories. In this case, it was part of the same HQ Division complex on Ogilvie Road that housed my own office in the Security Service. As Silver and I walked out of our own building and over to 'the lab' I was hoping that this meeting would answer my questions about the 'suspicious package' that Silver had identified as containing explosives.

Identifying myself at their main reception desk, I explained that I'd been requested for a meeting. After only a few minutes, I spotted a somewhat elderly-looking man coming down the main staircase to greet me. At the sight of him, I had to suppress a smile. Dr. Barry McDecy, Ph.D., FCIC was white-haired, slow moving, and wore a knitted sweater or vest underneath an unbuttoned, white lab-coat. My first thoughts flashed back to some of the chemistry professors of my university days. My reminiscences, however, evaporated at the sound of his hearty voice and a handshake that would have crushed my hand if I hadn't been taught the proper way to receive a handshake[13].

"Barry McDecy. Pleased to meet you," he said. "Your boss tells me that you trained as a chemist yourself?"

"Yes," I nodded. "I majored in analytical chemistry under professor Alan Grey at Carleton[14]."

"Excellent," he said, rubbing his hands energetically. "I understand that you're interested in the bomb that the OPP found last week."

"So it actually was a bomb?"

"Oh, yes. Yes. It's an exciting find – something new – and although there's still work to be done, I can tell you quite a bit about it already. Let's go up to my office, grab some coffee, and I'll fill you in." All this came out in a rush, as he'd already turned and was heading up the stairs much more quickly than he'd come down.

"OK then. You'll have learned the basics of homemade bomb-making when the two of you trained at Innisfail[15]," he said, after we'd supplied ourselves with coffee (and a bowl of water for Silver, which I thought was a considerate touch) and were seated comfortably in Barry's office. "So you know that any explosive device, no matter how simple or complicated, needs an oxidizer, a fuel, and a way to detonate it…. Now then, any explosive device is at least somewhat sensitive to heat, shock, friction, and electrostatic discharge, which enables a variety of different ways of managing the detonation, but which also make the devices hazardous to the bomb-maker…. In 1970, for example, an amateur-bomb-making operation in a Greenwich Village townhouse blew-up. Two of the bomb-makers were killed by the explosion, while a third died when the house collapsed on him[16]."

Although Barry glanced at me to make sure I was paying attention, he didn't need any comments from me: he was on a roll.

"So, your typical amateur bomb-maker leads a risky life and has a short life-expectancy. But," he held up the index finger of his right hand for emphasis, "in this case we have something different. Something new." His eyes lit up again at this point. "I was able to go over and meet the OPP bomb squad at Natural Resources Canada's (NRCan's) explosives testing and disposal range[17]. I had to do some fast talking but, in the end, they let me cut into the two plastic bottles and take small samples from each. After that they took the device into one of their test/disposal areas, had everyone back away, and then a police marksman detonated it from a safe distance with a single rifle shot."

"A rifle shot?"

"Yes. Obviously one bottle was filled with a mixture that could be set off by a shock wave. The second one was simply extra fuel and, man, the force of the explosion was something to behold. The first bottle contained the primary explosive, that's why it had a bright orange cap, to make it a visible target for a rifle shot from a safe distance away. A safe enough distance not to get caught in the blast, but, more importantly, a safe enough distance to make it easy to get away without being noticed by anyone. The OPP told me later that several residents that lived near the scene of the derailment all agreed that there was a crack like a rifle-shot right before the first explosion. One witness, a military veteran, thinks that crack sounded like a high-calibre rifle shot; like a .303 maybe, or possibility a .45 or .455.... But I'm getting side-tracked. Now then, here's the interesting part, I think it was a binary explosive!"

"Binary?"

"Right, binary. What you do is, you make up one bottle with some of the needed components and a second bottle with the rest. If it's done right, neither bottle would be considered explosive by itself, but when they're mixed together, all that's missing is something to set it off. Something like, say, the shock wave from a rifle bullet. The idea has been around for a while, but I've never heard of a homemade device like this, and the one I saw definitely looked homemade. I'm still working out the details of how it must have been done, but now you know the gist of it."

"Right. So, a pair of bottles that are easy and safe to transport and store, followed by a final mixture that can be detonated by a rifle located a long distance away."

"That's right."

"But Silver was still able to detect this one and identify it as being explosive. Would he have been able to detect and identify the separate bottles before the mixing?"

"I'll have to get back to you on that, but for now, I think so. I gathered some residue samples after the device had been detonated at the NRCan testing range, and I compared them with the residue samples that were gathered at the derailment site. The explosive-related residues from both locations match, and I've been able to identify some of the original components. The rest I'm still working on.

"What I can tell you for now, is that theses devices were variations on the fertilizer bomb idea."

"Ammonium nitrate," I said, automatically.

"Correct, so if you ever come across another of these things, and it's before mixing, then one of the bottles will contain ammonium nitrate, along with a few other things. Silver should be able to identify that one. The other bottle: well, I'm not entirely sure yet."

From there, Barry went on to describe what else he thought would be in 'bottle number one' as he called it, and what he thought was probably in 'bottle number two' and we talked chemistry for a while. Eventually, Barry ran out of steam and I thanked him for filling me in on what he learned so far.

"Happy to be of service," he replied, with a twinkle in his eye. "Come back another time, and we'll talk about the latest analytical methods we're bringing in and the price-tags on some of our latest instruments! The Commissioner is going to have a fit when he sees the cost of the GC-MS[18] I want to buy next."

A few days later, there was another surprise. I'd been in Bob's office discussing a different case with him, and when we'd exhausted that topic, he changed the subject. "Remember the bombing that caused the derailment and fire you were called-out to?"

"I doubt that I'll ever forget it," I replied. "That was the biggest fire I've ever seen. Why?"

"There's been a new development. Have a look at this." He passed over a clear plastic folder containing a single page on which mismatched letters had been cut out and glued, along with a picture of a fire.

"THIS IS ONLY THE BEGINNING," it read.

"The envelope is there too, in the back of the folder," Bob continued. "As you can see, it was simply addressed to RCMP Headquarters, Ottawa. It arrived yesterday and was immediately sent over to the lab so a document examiner could look at it. He should be here any minute."

"Someone with a grudge, or a cause, maybe?" I mused.

"Possibly. But it's interesting that it was sent to us rather than to a media outlet, like the CBC, for example. I suspect that our villain wants to play games with us, or get caught by us, or both."

"Wonderful," I commented. "Like, a serial murderer, or a serial arsonist, but maybe worse."

"Exactly."

We were interrupted in our musing by the arrival of the document examiner from the forensic lab.

"Hi Gerry," said Bob, in response to a knock on his door, and I was introduced to Gerald Tate, a civilian member of the Force and an expert document examiner. Gerry was tall and slender, with wire-rimmed glasses and a head full of thick, long hair. He looked too young to be a document examiner, but I found out later that he'd done a degree in mathematics before joining the Force, and had already put in the years apprenticing to an expert forensic document examiner that were required to get certified himself. *Maybe I'm getting old*, I thought to myself.

"I don't have much for you to go on, I'm afraid," Gerry began. "We're looking at very plain, standard paper, envelope, and glue. The paper is quite clean. So much so, that I suspect its author wore gloves while doing the gluing. There were prints on the back of the paper, but they were well enough wiped that I can't even pick up a partial print. The envelope was postmarked in Winnipeg and, of course, is covered in fingerprints. I've taken images of each of them, and eliminated those of the mailroom handler that received the letter, but the rest have most likely come from the postal handlers along the way."

"Winnipeg," mused Bob. "Could mean they're heading west. Anything else?"

"Just the letters themselves. They were all cut from the front covers of *Macleans Magazine* issues that were published between August and November of this year. The only letter our bomber couldn't get from those covers was a B, so the top half of an R was cut out and pasted upside down over the bottom of another R – you can see that the bottom half of the B wasn't aligned very carefully. Otherwise, that's all I've found so far."

"Thanks Gerry. From the tone of the message, I suspect we'll be getting another one of these, which may give you a bit more to work with."

"Sure. Just let me know," said Gerry, on his way out.

"I know he looks like a kid, but he knows his stuff," said Bob, as if having read my earlier thoughts. "If you get to know him, you'll find that he's a flexible thinker and has a good sense of humour."

"Well, that's good. I'd rather have my job and be out in the field than have his and be stuck in a lab all day, every day…. So you think they'll be more letters like this?"

"Seems likely. If our bomber is really heading west, that leaves a big part of the country and lots of inviting targets."

"And we just have to wait for the next bomb, and then maybe the next?"

"I'm afraid so. At least until we can detect a pattern, or the bomber gets more specific, or makes a mistake. In the meantime, all we can do is wait and keep an ear to the ground for any intelligence that might pop up."

Another mystery. Oh well, maybe I'll be able to read about it some day, I thought, as I was leaving Bob's office.

I was wrong, of course. I would never go back and read about it because it was going to grab me and drag me along with it.

3 THE SECOND CALL

Wednesday, December 5, 1979
Innisfail, Alberta

Two weeks later, the bombing and train derailment episode was a fading memory as Silver and I found ourselves back at the RCMP Dog Service Training Centre, which is located on its own grounds just outside of Innisfail, Alberta, a small, quiet town located a couple of miles south of the city of Red Deer and about seventy miles north of Calgary. It was nice to be back in sight of the Rocky Mountains, which lay due west.

This was where Silver and I had done our basic police dog and handler training[19], which took about four months, after which we'd stayed on for explosives training. It had been a bit uncomfortable at first because Silver and I were so different from what they had been used to.

We'd been inserted into the program outside of their normal selection process for dog handlers, I was the first woman to train as a dog handler, and Silver, being an Alaskan Malamute, is not their usual choice of breed. It probably didn't help that when any of these topics came up, I'd been ordered to simply say that I was a pilot project[20] of Assistant Commissioner MacLeod's, and to refer questions to his office.

In this case, my worries had been unfounded. I'd found the Police Dog Service (PDS) group to be a relaxed, engaging, and close-knit group and had really enjoyed my time there. These and many more such memories came back to me as we turned off the highway and into the compound. When Silver and I checked-in at

25

the main office my former instructor, Bill Preston, immediately came over to greet us.

"Except for those Corporal's stripes, you haven't changed a bit Alex," he said, trying to look around Silver who was standing up on his hind legs, fore-legs positioned squarely on Bill's chest, and his tongue licking every part of Bill's face he could get at. "Congratulations!"

"Thank you, Bill. It's great to see you again, and congratulations are in order for you as well I see," I looked pointedly at the Staff Sergeant's stripes on his uniform.

"Yes, you can't make fun of old 'Sergeant Preston' anymore."

This was a reference to the fictional *Sergeant Preston of the Yukon* series of radio and television shows that were broadcast from the late 1930s through to the mid-1950s. Bill didn't seem to have changed much either in the three years since I'd last seen him. He was medium height, lean, and soft-spoken, and my first impressions of him had been that he was very much like the Hollywood stereotype of a cowboy.

"Thank you for accepting our invitation to speak at our dinner tonight."

"You're welcome. I was surprised to be asked."

"Well, everyone in the Force gets transferred around the country from time to time, but with your job you've probably spent more time running around different parts of the country than any other dog master. Plus, you have to admit you've had some pretty exciting and successful cases beyond the normal tracking of lost kids and escaping suspects that occupy most of PDS team's time. I'm looking forward to hearing some of your stories myself."

"I understand that it will mostly be new people that I'll be talking to?"

"Mostly, yes. Some are very new, others aren't new to the Force but they're new to PDS, and a few have experience but are back here for specialty training or re-training. A bit of a mixed bunch, but they'll be hanging on every word. With your Security Service work and your undercover cases, you're beginning to get a reputation as a kind of female James Bond, you know."

"I know," I made a face. "It's not even slightly accurate you know, I'd rather have a licence-to-save than a licence-to-kill, and my most exciting moments have also been the most terrifying. Besides, I don't like vodka martinis, shaken or stirred."

"That's OK," said Bill, "but you're always going to be a hero around here." Then, seeing my discomfort, he changed the subject back to business. "How about if I tour you around, show you some of the changes we've made around here, and then after lunch there'll be a bit of a graduation and demonstration event. The public have been invited, so there should be a decent-sized crowd to watch the new graduates show-off their skills, a few demonstrations with the specialists, and then a brief graduation ceremony."

"Sounds great."

As we walked around the grounds, I noticed that there were several teams working at various places like the obstacle courses and so forth. I could tell at a glance which were the experienced teams and which the not so experienced or, in one case at least, the obviously brand new. The latter was quite amusing and I had to stifle a laugh and turn my head away so as not to risk embarrassing the novice dog handler whose new partner was ignoring him completely.

"Quite the spectrum, hmmm?" said Bill, who noticed everything.

"Brings back memories, too," I agreed, except that my attention had been caught by a very cohesive-looking team that appeared to be doing some kind of search exercise off by the perimeter of the compound. The dog, a German Shepherd, was digging at something that must have been at least partly in the ground while the handler, who had her back to me, was shouting out instructions and encouragement. There was something about that woman that kept nagging at the corner of my mind and causing me to look back at her even as Bill and I had turned to look at another part of the compound.

"Something wrong?" asked Bill.

"Not wrong, but there's something about that woman over there. Something familiar, but I can't put my finger on it. Who is she?"

But, before Bill could reply the woman turned towards me. When I saw her profile a lump formed in my throat, and when I saw her face, I was sure.

"Julie?" I whispered. "It can't be Julie...."

Just then she obviously saw me too, because she immediately yelled "Alex!!" and came towards us, followed closely by her dog.

She would be in her mid-twenties now, I thought, but she still had a blond ponytail sticking out of the back of her baseball cap, and just as alive and energetic as she jogged over to where we were standing. As she approached, she threw her arms wide and engulfed me in a huge hug. "It's so great to see you again!"

"It's wonderful to see you, but I can't believe it. How did you get here, and how did you get into the Force?"

Turning to Bill, I added, "Julie and I worked together in Alaska searching for a lost Girl Guide[21], but she was a Park Ranger then, in Alaska's Klondike Gold Rush National Historic Park. An American Park Ranger."

"Well, there's not too much to tell," she said with the cheery smile and sparkling blue eyes I remembered so well. "Remember how I always wanted to do something useful but all my male supervisors ever wanted me to do was organize coffee and doughnuts? Well, working with you and Silver was exciting, and rewarding, and the only time I ever got to do anything useful, so I decided to quit and try to be like you. My father is in the Canadian military, and I was born when he was stationed at the NORAD[22] base in Colorado Springs. That gave me dual citizenship, so I was eligible for the U.S. National Park Service as an American and the RCMP as a Canadian. Both the Park Service and the Skagway Chief of Police gave me good references when I applied, and the Force let me in. As soon as I could I transferred into PDS, and here I am."

"You should have let me know."

"I wanted to, but I wanted to get in on my own, and I wanted to surprise you," she paused then, and gave Bill a knowing look.

"It was Julie that suggested you as our after-dinner speaker tonight. We all thought it was a great idea, and I'll admit that I enjoyed going along with the surprise part."

"*Grruph*," said Silver, at this point. While we'd been talking, Silver and the big German Shepherd had been greeting and sniffing at each other.

It had begun with the two dogs spotting each other, and then looking very directly at each other as they approached. When they were about 10 metres (30 ft) away, low growls could be heard from each of them. This was followed by more staring, as each took a few more steps forward. I'd been watching them closely while Julie and I were speaking and I'd just about decided to speak to Silver. I wasn't needed, however. As if some kind of inaudible conversation had been taking place, Julie's dog suddenly bowed down, placing his forelegs out in front of him and his head low to the ground. At this, Silver gave a kind of yip and Julie's dog got back up so the two of them could approach each other closely enough to sniff at each other. This was followed by the usual sequence of sniffing around each other's noses, then each other's butts, with much slow circling. It was kind of like a dance of acquaintance and acceptance, I thought.

"That went well," said Julie, who had also been watching them out of the corner of her eye.

"Yes, and without either of us having to say a word or intervene."

"So, meet Scout. He's 16 months old."

"Hello, Scout," I said, going down on one knee to offer a hand for him to sniff.

"RR*uff*," said Scout, looking up at me after taking several good sniffs.

"Scout?" I said to Julie, as I stood back up.

Scout and Silver

"Well, I figured that if Silver could be named after the Lone Ranger's horse, then Scout could be named after Tonto's, and I'm hoping he'll be my 'faithful friend.'"

"Julie and Scout have done really well here," put in Bill, "and you'll see them in action during the demonstrations this afternoon."

"Speaking of which, we have a few things to do before the public get here, so I'll see you later. OK?" As I nodded, she and Scout trotted off.

"Surprised?" asked Bill.

"I'm amazed. It's hard to believe she's even in Canada much less that she's joined the Force."

"And PDS."

"Yes that too but, come to think of it, she was very impressed with Silver and with the amount of independence a dog master gets."

"You two sound like 'birds of a feather.'"

"Kindred spirits, that's for sure," I agreed.

"Ah ha," said Bill, "another *Anne of Green Gables*[23] reader. Didn't the Anne Shirley character have red hair too?" he asked, rather slyly.

"Oh yes, and before you say it, an independent spirit as well."

Chuckling, Bill said "Come on and I'll show you the rest of the changes we've made around here."

After showing me around the grounds, Bill led us inside for lunch and to warm up. A few of the other instructors joined us as well – all new since Silver and I had trained there.

"Yes, there are a few old hands like me still around," said Bill when I asked about this. "You'll see some of them at the public demonstrations and then later tonight."

After lunch, we went outside to find that a sizeable crowd was gathering for the public event, which was to be a combination of dynamic displays by the handlers and their dogs, demonstrating a variety of skills and techniques, followed by a fairly short, informal graduation ceremony for the new PDS teams.

Although it was early December and there was snow on the ground, a strong Chinook[24] wind was blowing out from the Rocky Mountains to the west of us, making it warm enough to be outside – for a while, anyway – but I got the feeling that bad weather wouldn't have deterred much of the crowd, which seemed to be largely made up of families and friends of the new graduates.

It was not only nice to sit and watch the handlers and their dogs show off their skills, it brought back a lot of memories for me, and I found myself stroking Silver's shoulder fur as the remembrances came back. When Julie and Scout were doing their routines, I felt as captivated and proud as the families around us.

When the show was over, everyone was invited to go indoors for a warm-up and refreshments. Silver and I hung back, hoping to congratulate Julie, who turned out to be on the far side of the neatly lined-up rows of chairs, away from the building to which the crowd was heading. As a result, by the time we got to her, most of the crowd had left and we were essentially alone.

"Congratulations Julie!" I said, when we met up, "and to you too Scout," I added, looking directly into his eyes as I did so.

Julie's "Thanks," and Scout's "*RRuff*," came out at the same time, which got us laughing. It was starting to feel like old times being there with her.

Something strange happened as we were walking over to join the rest of the crowd, however. Julie and I were chatting away as we made our way along an empty row of chairs that was roughly in the middle of the seating area when Silver suddenly lifted his head and began sniffing in the direction of the back rows. He seemed serious, so I stopped in mid-sentence and said, "What is it Silver?"

"*Grruph*," he said, still sniffing and staring intently towards the back rows of chairs.

"Trouble?" asked Julie, who had seen Silver in actions years before.

"I don't know, but the most important lesson I learned when I trained here was: 'Pay attention to what the dog is trying to tell you,' and it's never let me down."

Just then, Silver began to tug at his leash. I normally use a long lead, when I use one at all, with the extra rope coiled up in one hand. I released it, and without waiting for instructions he immediately led us between chairs, across the rows, heading for the rear. We'd really only cut across a single row, when Scout suddenly said "*RRuff*," and began to tug at his leash. As Julie released him, both dogs advanced slowly looking, or rather, sniffing this way and that as if searching for a weak scent whose origin was difficult to locate.

"Did you and Scout take any special training while you were here, or just the basic course?" I asked, as we waited to see whether the dogs would be able to track down whatever had aroused their interest.

"Well, we came here to do the basic course but then someone suddenly decided to let us stay on. I think there must have been a cancellation that created a last-minute hole, and we just happened to be on the waiting list for the course anyway."

"What course?"

"Oh, explosives, of course! Just like you two."

"Uh oh," I said.

"No!" said Julie, catching my train of thought. "Surely not here, of all places?"

"I think we're going to find out pretty soon."

Soon was right. Within seconds, Silver and Scout had come from different directions to converge on the same chair, give another sniff, and then sit on their haunches and look directly at Julie and I.

"What'd you find Silver?" I asked, as I approached and bent down on one knee to look. It took a second to realize what I was looking at, and then I knew. "Oh no!"

"What is it?" asked Julie, who'd come up just behind and beside me.

I sighed. "I think it's a new kind of bomb. I saw one like it in Ontario last month with the same bright orange cap on one of two bottles taped together. If I'm right, that bottle has the explosive and the other one contains extra fuel."

"Where's the detonator then?" asked Julie, carefully looking but not touching.

"If it's what I think it is, there's no timer and no detonator here. It gets set off by the shock wave from a high-calibre rifle bullet. The orange cap acts as a high-visibility target. It's strange though, because if there was a shooter over there somewhere...." I pointed along an imaginary line tangent to the face of the orange cap, which led directly towards the demonstration area, "the target surely wouldn't be visible."

"Look! I bet that's a note," said Julie, pointing to an envelope that had been taped to the seat of the chair.

After making sure that there were no wires attached to the envelope, or to the chair for that matter, I reached for the envelope and pulled it away. I doubted that there were any fingerprints on it, but I used a handkerchief and handled as carefully as I could anyway. Using my Swiss Army knife, I slit the envelope and extracted the contents – a single sheet of paper. After unfolding the letter, for that's what it was, I sighed and held it up for Julie to read.

It was a short letter, made up of cut-out letters pasted to the page.

"RCMP. HERE WE GO AGAIN. CATCH ME," it read.

"I take it you've also seen letters like this one before?" asked Julie, after a glance at my sour expression.

"Just one, but there's a connection. I don't know whether the bomb is live or just a dummy with the right scent, but either way it's been put here as a message."

The rest of the afternoon and early evening were consumed by next steps. With Julie and Scout standing guard, I had taken Silver to find and alert Bill, who had taken command of the situation. The area was cordoned off to a distance of 365 m (1,200 ft) in all directions[25], the public evacuated from the training centre, and a call was placed with the Calgary Police Service bomb squad. While that was going on, I had placed a call to Ottawa, asking my boss Bob to get someone high-up in the Calgary force's chain of command to ensure that the bomb squad took the device to a secure place but did NOT purposely explode it until we could get a forensic explosives expert to look at it.

Later, instead of the planned PDS dinner and my after-dinner speech (both of which were cancelled) the evening found us in Bill's backyard eating take-out food: just Bill, his wife, Julie, and myself, while Silver and Scout ate and played with Bill's retired PSD Mike. While we ate, I related the story of the train derailment, the two bombs, and the first letter.

"The characters on the first letter were all cut from the front covers of *Macleans Magazine* issues between August and November of this year. Do you have any recent copies of *Macleans* ?" I asked.

Bill's wife, Carol, went to look and shortly came back with the most recent, December 3, issue.

"Looks like at least some of the letters came from this cover all right," said Bill, comparing the magazine to the letter.

Bill also explained that he'd had people searching for a potential shooter, without results, and other people questioning the visitors before they left. "No one seems to have noticed anything suspicious," he concluded, "and all we got from people that had been sitting near the chair with the envelope were vague recollections of a man, medium height, and slender build, with thin, fairly straight hair, greying and parted almost in the middle. Apparently came and went alone, didn't talk to anybody, and was carrying or wearing a daypack."

"Well, that's more than we knew before I guess," I offered. "The first letter suggested to us that more bombs would be planted, and we wondered whether the bomber was setting things up to prepare for an extortion attempt or some kind of psychological catch-me-if-you-can game. It looks like it's going to be the latter."

"Do you think you'll be assigned to the case?" asked Julie.

"I doubt it," I said slowly, thinking about it as I spoke. "It's domestic terrorism and it's crossed provinces, so it'll land with the Security Service for sure, but I imagine Uncle George will wait until there's more to go on before assigning specific resources to this one. It would be like looking for a needle in a haystack without knowing what a needle looks like, or which haystack to search." Then I noticed the amused expression on Bill's face.

"Uncle George?" he asked.

"Oops, I mean the A/C." For Julie's benefit, I added, "We're talking about Assistant Commissioner George MacLeod, the head of the Security Service. Some of the staff refer to him as 'The Old Man,' the same as if he was the CO of a Division, but my immediate boss, Bob, and I refer to him as Uncle George. We always figured that if we were ever found out, we'd claim it was a code name for security reasons, but the truth is that its because he looks after us like family and that's a nice feeling to have if you're out, all by yourself, working under cover."

"You think he's the head of the Security Service and he doesn't know what you call him behind his back?" asked Bill incredulously.

"He quite likely knows very well, but pretends not to know," I agreed, "but everything is played like a game in intelligence work, with games within games, and so on until you think you're going crazy. I bet he knows full well that it's a term of endearment too, but he'll never admit that either – it would be bad for discipline."

That brought a few chuckles that were interrupted by the ringing of the telephone, which Carol got up and went inside the house to answer. She returned in only moments.

"I think they heard you out in Ottawa, Alex. It's for you, a Staff Sergeant Simpson."

"My boss," I said, "maybe he'll have some news for us."

I was on the phone for some time, and although I returned to the sounds of happy chatting and laughing, it all ceased when they saw the serious look on my face.

"More trouble," said Bill. It was a statement rather than a question, and he was right.

"I think so. Another letter was delivered to HQ this afternoon. It said: "TRANS-MTN IS NEXT: IN AB.""

"What does that mean?" asked Julie.

"There's a large oil pipeline, called the Trans Mountain Pipeline[26], that runs between the refinery district in Edmonton and Burnaby, BC, which has a storage and distribution terminal. Bob thinks the bomber is saying he's going to hit the pipeline somewhere along the Alberta side."

"If he sent a note to Ottawa, then why bother leaving one here in Innisfail?" asked Julie.

"I don't know. Bob's idea is that he knows that dog teams are trained here to search for explosives, and the letter we got here today challenges us to find him, so maybe it's all part of his 'I'm smarter than the police are,' or 'I want to be caught' game."

"But that's crazy. Sooner or later we'll get him and people will get hurt."

"That's why Bob's decided we have to start doing something. To begin with, he's assigning two people to the case. If they can develop some more leads, or if more letters arrive, then more resources will be added along the way."

"Sounds like a waste of time to me. That's a lot of distance to cover. The Alberta portion of the pipeline runs from Edmonton to just past Jasper. That's 350 km, with lots of wide-open spaces along the way. Two people patrolling that distance could check an area one day, find it clear, and then have the bomber strike the same location the very next day, after they're gone. Finding him would be like trying to buy a winning lottery ticket. Do you know what poor saps they're going to saddle this one with?" Then Bill saw the look on my face. "Oh, no!"

"Oh yes," I said. "Bob says I'm to be the poor sap and what's more, I'm to be in charge. He agrees the odds of accomplishing much more are slim at this point, but that we can't afford to sit back anymore doing nothing. He says that, if nothing else, this will give me a chance to try supervising a constable, something I've never done before."

"Well, that should be useful anyway," allowed Bill. "Good thinking on his part. Do you know who he's going to assign to you?"

"Actually, he said my first task as supervisor is to decide what kind of help to ask for and he'd try to arrange it. I thought of asking for Jack McDonald because we've worked so well together on previous cases[27], but then I had another idea. What if I could get another PDS team with an explosives-trained dog...."

At that, Julie sat up straight in a flash, saying "Can Scout and I come?"

"I think so. Bob says he'll find out where you were supposed to be assigned next and talk to Uncle George about getting you temporarily attached to this job for as long as it takes to find this guy. He says that if Uncle George throws his weight around, we should have a telex confirmation by mid-day tomorrow."

"I can't believe it. This is exactly what I hoped for when I signed up," said Julie.

"This isn't going to be fun and games, you know," I said, rather sternly. Then, seeing the excitement die out of Julie's face I relented a bit. "But I'm looking forward to it too, and I'm going to be very glad to have you and Scout with us."

"I still think it's crazy," said Bill, "but good luck to you both!"

4 INVESTIGATING

Meanwhile, the man calling himself Frank Smith had been fairly busy. After the Ontario bombings, he repainted the truck – flat black this time, as he could only hand-spray-paint it in flat colours and produce a look that wasn't too obviously done by an amateur. The truck's box, he covered with a used, white fibreglass cap that he had purchased for cash in a private sale. To complete the transformation, he switched licence plates again using the same method he had previously used in Alberta. He found an industrial site with a large employee parking lot, removed a complete set of front and rear plates from a vehicle, and then removed the front plate from an adjacent vehicle and placed it on the rear of the first one. If anyone had chanced to see his vehicle parked near the scene of the train derailment and noted the colour and licence plates, the police would now be misdirected long enough for him to leave the province. At least, he hoped so.

Driving west, he mailed the first anonymous letter when he stopped overnight in Winnipeg, Manitoba. The next two days saw him drive to Saskatoon and then north to beyond Prince Albert, where he had a hunting and trapping cabin tucked away among the tall aspen and white spruce of the northern boreal forest. With the end of November fast approaching the air temperature was -10 °C (14 °F) and dropping, so the first thing he did was to open the cabin, check that everything was in order, and light the cast-iron stove.

This done, he emerged from the cabin and stopped to look and listen for a few moments to make sure there was no one around. Then, satisfied, he retrieved a shovel from a small shack on the property. At one corner of the rear of his cabin, on the outside, he knelt down, cleared away the snow, and began to dig. He didn't have to dig far. About 30 cm (1 ft) down, his shovel struck metal. *It's still there*, he thought, sighing with relief. It took only a few minutes more to dig away enough dirt to expose the rugged, .50 calibre army surplus ammunition case and lever it up from its hiding place.

There was no lock to open, the box's security had been its secret hiding place. Lifting the lever-latch he opened the lid, exposing several envelopes of documents, several bundles of paper money, some keys, a gold pocket watch and chain, and a handful of gold coins. Removing the bundles of currency, he stuffed them into an inner jacket pocket, ignored everything else, and closed and latched the box. This, he placed back in the hole, and replaced all the dirt. After smoothing-out the surface dirt, he got up, and took the shovel back to the shed. While there, he scavenged around the area for a couple of handfuls of fallen leaves, needles, and fine branch ends, which he took back to where he had been digging. Scattering his handfuls of collected debris over the freshly levelled dirt he made it look as undisturbed as possible, then replaced the snow cover.

Stepping back from the cabin, he surveyed his work. Everything was in order saving the holes in the snow where he had been digging and where he had walked. Fortunately, the snow was quite fresh and powdery with no hard, frozen crust on top. Selecting a fallen tree branch from near the shed, and walking backwards, he used the branch like a broom to smooth out the snow in the entire area from the shed to the back of the cabin, and around the side to the front. As he surveyed his work, he noted that it would be obvious to anyone that there had been some kind of activity there, but no one was likely to come this way any time soon and over time wind, dropping leaves and branches, and the next snowstorm would cover everything.

Between the non-perishable supplies stocked in his cabin and what he had with him in the truck there was enough to eat and drink so that he could stay overnight and drive south the next day.

Over the next several days, he drove south to Saskatoon, then west to Edmonton, Alberta, where he found an inexpensive place to stay in the north (industrial) end of town. There, he looked up all the nearby agricultural chemical and metal finishing and plating type businesses in the local area and spent the next two days carefully checking each one, literally inside and out. He had learned everything he knew about bomb-making from a fellow inmate at the penitentiary, who claimed to be the inventor of the binary explosive devices. The bomb maker had traded this knowledge for Frank's lessons in wood- and metalworking. It was the bomb maker who had recommended the specific commercial products Frank could obtain from agricultural supply and metal finishing and plating businesses. Fortunately for Frank, just like the Niagara area in Southern Ontario, Edmonton had several of both kinds of businesses to choose from. His only other immediate task was to construct another anonymous letter, which he mailed to the RCMP in Ottawa.

Having selected one of each kind of business, based on his assessments that they had the poorest security of their kind in the area, he broke into each on successive nights of a single weekend.

There was at least 15 cm (6 in) of snow on the ground, so he had purchased a pair of oversized army-surplus felt-pack boots to use, so that the footprints he left in the snow were both commonplace and larger than his normal boot size. In addition, in each case he had parked more than a kilometre away from the business to avoid his truck being seen and associated with the crimes and, in each case, he only stole amounts of chemical that he could easily conceal about his person and carry away. In one case, the cash register hadn't been emptied at the end of the day. "That's going to cost you," he thought to himself, as he scooped up nearly $500.

With the proceeds of these two latest robberies, plus the supplies in his truck, he had enough material to make three more bombs. This would be his task for the next day or two, and it was purely by accident that he read in the Edmonton newspaper about the public event that was to be held at the RCMP's dog training centre in Innisfail.

Hmmm, he thought to himself, *Azrael must be watching over me*[28]. *I bet they train explosives-sniffing dogs there. This could be a good opportunity to find out whether an explosives-trained dog can detect my binary-type bombs.* He decided to make another anonymous letter.

***

Frank's visit to the RCMP's dog training facility at Innisfail had been nerve-wracking. Despite blending-in with the crowd, he had been keenly aware of the presence of the dogs, at least one of whom would surely have been trained in explosives detection. He'd reasoned that the afternoon's events would hold everyone's attention, especially that of the dog handlers and their dogs, but he also knew that he was taking a big risk. Fortunately for him, he'd had no trouble securing a seat near the rear of the seating area and he'd been able to unobtrusively plant the bomb and the next letter while everyone's attention was focused elsewhere.

He had never intended to actually detonate this particular bomb, which was simply another demonstration, so all he had to do was watch the events like everyone else, and then leave the seating area with everyone else. The only difference was that while almost everyone else went to search-out and congratulate the relatives or friends they'd come to celebrate, he simply walked to his truck and drove away.

Back in his Edmonton hotel room, he reviewed his plans. The next event concerned the pipeline threatened in his third letter. He had already constructed several addition bombs, but he needed to prepare the next letter – letter number four. When that was finished, he drove west of the city to find the Stony Plain pump station and reconnoitre. Once there, he stayed away from the pump station itself and instead drove down each of the surrounding and connecting roads seeking a location that would provide good cover yet a good line-of-sight for him to observe the station, a place to conceal his truck, and easy access to roads that could be used to get away in a hurry, should that become necessary. There were so many clumps and rows of trees and bushes dotting the landscape that he had no difficulty selecting two locations that he thought would meet his needs. He decided to leave the final decision until later.

Frank figured that the RCMP would send a dog handler and dog from Innisfail for the simple reasons that the RCMP only had a few explosives-trained dogs in any one province, and that there were probably only one or two such teams near Edmonton, and perhaps only one or two that would have been at Innisfail and therefore have seen the actual device, so the latter handler (or handlers) would be the only ones in the region that knew what the devices look like. Furthermore, if the RCMP was taking his threats as seriously as they should, then they would send a team from Innisfail to search the exposed segments of the pipeline, beginning at the front-end in Edmonton, or the first pump station, which was at Stony Plain. As it turned out, Frank's reasoning in all these things was quite sound, including his guess that the first location to be searched would be the one at Stony Plain if for no other reason than the fact that it would inevitably have less robust security than the much larger Edmonton facility. The largest question in Frank's mind was therefore not whether, or where, but when?

It was Thursday, December 6th. The public event at Innisfail had been the day before, by which time the third letter should have been received in Ottawa. If the RCMP promptly sent a team to search, they would probably begin on the Friday or, if the letter arrived late then the Saturday or Sunday. That meant he had to plant the bomb and letter right away and then maintain a watching vigil for the next three days to see if anyone turned up to search. He decided to make his move just before sunset, when things should be quiet at the pump station and visibility would be poor but with sufficient natural light for him to move around. Satisfied, he drove back to town to rest.

Later that same evening Frank drove back to the pump station. He was wearing medium-dark-coloured clothes and had a scarf tied around his face and his hood pulled up. The colours of his clothes were chosen so as to make it difficult for the black-and-white security cameras to resolve his image when he was stationary, and not much more of his appearance when he was in motion. He estimated, correctly, that the pipeline company would have a control room somewhere with multiple monitors on which live images from the many pump stations along the line would be rotated from time to time. Since there were more than twenty locations to monitor, he thought the chances of being spotted were slim. Nevertheless, he parked his truck near one corner of the compound at which there was one of two security cameras that he'd identified during his earlier reconnaissance. If any kind of alarm went off, he wanted the truck close by so he could get away quickly.

The corner security camera he'd chosen was mounted on a pole at about five metres (15 ft) off the ground. He scaled the fence and then stood on its top with one hand on the pole so he could maintain his balance. From inside his parka, he withdrew a collapsible ski pole which he now extended, being careful to secure its three concentric sections in the fully extended position using the screw fittings provided. With his free hand, he used the ski pole to slowly make the security camera rotate to one side – not a lot, just enough so that the camera would still record a view of the pump station, but not the part he was planning to approach. With luck, the change would either not be noticed for a while, or else an operator would suspect a bird strike and make a note for a repair technician to go and fix it.

Without collapsing the ski pole, Frank then jumped down from the fence to land on the outside of the compound again, and worked his way around to the corner of the compound on which he'd spotted a second security camera. There he repeated his actions, again nudging the camera to change its field of view away from where he planned to go. This done, he jumped down, landing inside the compound this time, and walked over to the spot he'd chosen to plant the bomb and letter. Next, he went back to each camera location, scaled the fence again, and used his ski pole to nudge the cameras back to their original locations, or at least as close to that as he could judge. This way, the changes he'd earlier made might never be noticed at all, he figured.

With his evening's work complete, Frank made the long walk back to his truck. When he had the engine running, and the truck's heater giving off a welcome blast of hot air to alleviate the chill of being outdoors, he was satisfied. Now he had a bit of an ordeal to endure. He planned to spend the next three days, at least, watching the pump station from one of the two vantage points he'd selected. Both vantage points were a reasonable distance away, with good tree and brush cover, and right beside a range road with good access to several turn-offs to other range roads.

He already had field-glasses, a spotting-scope, and a good thermos from previous activities. Recently, he had additionally procured a groundsheet, a warm sleeping blanket, and a white sheet for winter-camouflage.

This would require patience.

It had been a fairly nice winter day on the Thursday when Frank had placed the bomb and letter, at +9 °C (48 °F),). That night, however, a cold front moved in dropping the temperature to an overnight low of -9 °C (16 °F). The next day, his first full day of surveillance, the temperature only warmed to a daytime high of -2° C (28 °F), making for a cold vigil, especially since nothing happened. The few pipeline staff that he saw seemed unaware of their security breach and no police showed up to search.

Saturday, his second day of surveillance, was only a little bit better, with the temperature warming to +2° C (36°F), but again there was nothing interesting for him to see beyond the occasional hawk out hunting.

By Sunday, his third day of surveillance, he was becoming frustrated and had begun to rethink his plan, when the police finally showed up at the pump station.

***

Bill had arranged for an office we could use, so the next morning I started making phone calls. The first was to Dr. Barry McDecy in the Ottawa forensic lab. He didn't have a lot more information about the components of the Ontario bomb, but when I told him what I had in mind he said: "Obviously ammonium nitrate, but that's easy to find. The other large component seems to have been perchlorate, probably ammonium perchlorate or maybe a mixture of perchlorates, but definitely perchlorate. That should narrow the field a bit."

Thanking him, I turned to Julie who had been hovering in the office hoping for something she could do to help. "OK, here's something you can do. Call CPIC[29] and ask them to run a stolen property search for some chemicals: ammonium nitrate, any other nitrates, ammonium perchlorate, and any other chlorates or perchlorates stolen any time since the beginning of September. That would take us back at least two months before the date of the first bombing."

"Great, I'll start right away," she said, happy to be doing something. "Where would you go to steal chemicals like these anyway?" she asked.

"Well, if it was me, I'd go to a university chemistry department because security is weak and I'd know exactly where to look. Someone without a science background would probably look in the chemical industry or for a business that uses such chemicals. If someone wanted huge quantities, they'd probably look for a chemical producer, or maybe an agricultural chemical supplier, for the nitrate at least. For perchlorates, maybe some kind of metal-smithing or metal-plating business. Anyway, don't get discouraged if nothing interesting comes up, we're going to have to regularly check into CPIC for as long as we're on the case."

"Ah ha, it's not just clues you're looking for but a pattern."

"At the moment, I'd be happy with either, but ultimately we'll probably need both if we're going to get anywhere."

That afternoon, we received two telex messages from Ottawa. The first, for Julie, had her new orders, attaching her to me for the duration of the case. The second, for me, stated that two unmarked police vehicles had been assigned to us and that they would be available for pick-up at K Division HQ, which was in Edmonton.

While Julie was busy working with CPIC and our queries, I called the head of security for the pipeline company. Many large companies hire retired police officers for their security team, to take advantage of their training and, in many cases, their networks. This company was no different, and I was transferred to a retired Staff Sergeant from the RCMP named Edward (Ed) Williams, who had considerable investigative experience. This was helpful because our common backgrounds helped us develop an early rapport, and he was able to immediately perceive the kinds of information I would need.

Ed explained that the Trans Mountain pipeline[30] consisted of approximately 1,150 kilometres (about 800 km) of pipe, most of which was of 24-inch (61 cm) diameter, with about 150 km each of 30-inch (76 cm) and 36-inch (91 cm) diameter pipe. "The good news is that the pipeline is buried underground for nearly the entire run. There are only a few places where it runs above ground, mostly when the pipe needs to come up at a pump station," he explained. "The bad news is that the pump stations are very exposed. We have eight active pump stations along the Alberta portion, between Edmonton and Jasper. These stations use electric pumps to keep the pipeline's 300,000 barrel per day capacity flowing[31]."

"Can you give me the locations?" I asked.

"You bet. The Alberta ones, beyond Edmonton, are at Stony Plain, Gainford, Chip, Wolf, Edson, Hinton, and Jasper."

"Are any of them more sensitive than the others?" I asked.

"Only in terms of media sensation if one of them blows," he said, after a moment's thought. "I mean, an explosion near Edmonton or one of the towns would cause more fear and panic, and greater media sensation. From an operating perspective though, no, if one pump station gets severely damaged or destroyed, the whole system comes to an immediate halt."

"OK. How about the explosive hazard?"

"Big. Doesn't matter what's in the line at the time. I'm no engineer, but we use what's called a batch-flow process. That means that different products can be individually shipped in batches. So, at any given place and time, the local run of pipe could be full of crude oil or one of its refined products. Obviously, the refined products are more flammable and a greater explosive hazard than raw crude oil, but that's the limit of my knowledge. All I know is that it would be bad no matter what's in the line. I can get you the technical specs if you want them."

"No, not right now anyway. I get your point about the hazard being large no matter what. Would it be possible to get a tour of one of these pump stations?"

"Surely. In fact, you can tour them all if you want. Where would you like to start? Security's pretty tight at our main Edmonton plant, and after what you've just told me, I'm going to tighten it even further. It's the remote sites I'm worried about."

"OK. We have a few things to do first in Edmonton, so how about if we begin with the Stony Plain station? Is there any chance we could see it three days from now? I know that's a Sunday...."

"Fine. Don't worry about it being a Sunday, as of now I'm on 24-hour call anyway, until this gets dealt with. Tell you what, that will give me time to brief our executives and put things in motion here, then I can drive up and show it to you myself. It will give us a chance to meet in person, which is important because I want you to trust me enough to tell me what's really going on as your investigation progresses. I'll share everything I have with you because it's important to my job, but I know from experience that you'll be naturally cautious about sharing with people you don't know."

I was suitably thankful, and said so. Based on first impressions over the phone, I was impressed with him too; he certainly seemed smart and capable.

Now that a plan was beginning to take shape I phoned my boss,

Bob, in Ottawa to update him and ask if he could arrange for a police plane[32] to take some aerial photographs for us.

"Probably," replied Bob. "What do you want and where?"

"The 'where' is the Trans Mountain pump station at Stony Plain, just outside of Edmonton. The 'what' are a series of low altitude, low-oblique[33] aerial photographs covering the surrounding area. I want to see if we can determine what kind of vehicle our bomber is using, but without the aircraft being obvious enough to scare him away."

"All right. I'll put them in the picture. They should be able to make a fly-past, then sweep around in a very broad circle, and then make a second fly-past along a different vector and at a different altitude. Anything more and they'll be spotted. Does that sound good enough."

"No, it doesn't, but I think it will have to be."

"OK then, when?"

I took a breath, and then said: "Beginning this afternoon, if possible. If not, then beginning tomorrow morning. I'm thinking we should get four flights a day: just after dawn, late morning, early to mid-afternoon, and then just before dusk. Then, fly the same patterns and schedule every day for a week."

There was silence for a moment as Bob wrote it all down and then paused to think about it. "You don't ask for much," he replied eventually.

"I know it's a long shot, and flight time is expensive but, so far, our bomber has been very careful and one step ahead of us. We need to turn up some clues."

I could hear a sigh over the phone line, and I imagined that Bob was thinking of all the red tape and fast-talking he was going to have to do. "OK Alex. You're the one in the field. I'll get it done."

I thanked him and breathed a sigh of relief. Even a long shot felt better than blindly following the bomber's notes around the country.

By the end of the day, Julie had progress to report on chemical thefts of potential interest to us.

"Here's what I've learned so far," she began, picking up a dry-erase marker and writing on the wall-mounted whiteboard[34]. The nitrates are easy to find, since Canada has agricultural chemical wholesalers and retailers in every province. The chlorates and perchlorates aren't as common. I thought we'd be looking for firework manufacturers, but it turns out that most of the world's fireworks are made in China and shipped here ready to go. The main companies that actually use chlorates in smallish quantities are metal polishing and electro-plating companies.

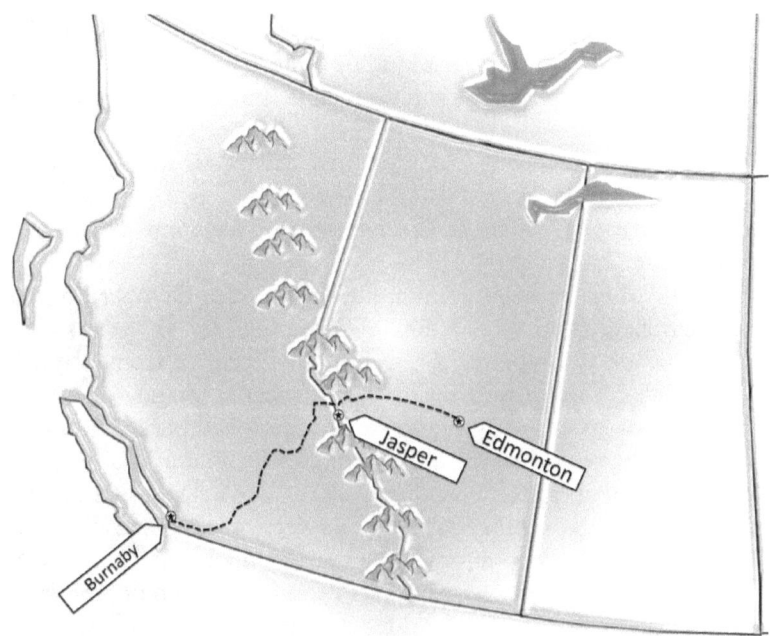

The Trans-Mountain Pipeline

"So, since the beginning of September, we have 33 reports of nitrate or chlorate thefts. If we limit the geography to central and western Canada, that reduces the number to 25. Now, if we further assume that our bomber doesn't want to carry around a lot of explosive materials then we can filter down to thefts that have been small, like only a few kilograms or less at a time, then we're down to 12."

"That's still quite a few hits," I muttered. I'd had the idea that fertilizer thefts would be few and far between, and even rarer for oxidizers.

"That's what I thought too, but then I noticed something unusual," she said, with a big smile. "A lot of the thefts involved multiple chemicals, but if we narrow the search down to just nitrates or just chromates, the list gets smaller, and some of the thefts on that smaller list were just one chemical."

"Suppose our bomber is only hitting smaller places with less security than the big ones, and suppose he's trying to be inconspicuous and is only taking small quantities that are easy to carry and conceal. No strange truck backed up at the rear of the store for someone to see. That kind of thing."

"OK," I said, "that's certainly possible, but that's making a lot of assumptions."

"I know," said Julie excitedly, "and I have a list we can look at that doesn't involve the extra assumptions. But, just for a moment, look what happens when we do make them. We come all the way down to four cases:

o 4 kg of calcium ammonium nitrate stolen in October, from a fertilizer company in Hamilton, Ontario,
o 3 kg of perchlorate, also stolen in October, from a metal polishing and plating business in Nepean, Ontario,
o 3 kg of ammonium nitrate stolen on November 29, from an agrochemical supplier in Spruce Grove, Alberta, and
o 2.5 kg of perchloric acid and $497.45 in cash stolen on the next day, November 30, from an electroplating and finishing business in Edmonton. The manager had gone home sick early that day, and the clerk had forgotten to empty the cash register before leaving and locking-up."

"That's amazing Julie. Hamilton isn't very far from Ottawa and Nepean is essentially right beside Ottawa, so those two could have provided the materials for the railway bombs. Spruce Grove is very close to Edmonton, so those last two could have provided the materials for yesterdays bombs, if it turns out that they were live, that is."

"Right. The two most recent ones, would have left him more than enough time to make a bomb, and another of those letters, and drive down here to Innisfail and place them."

"Well done, Julie!" I praised. "Keep all of your lists, but I think we should go to Edmonton tomorrow, pick up the vehicles they've set aside for us at K Division HQ, and go visit those last two businesses."

"Sounds good. Anything else?"

"Yes. While we're still here, would you please look into those two Ontario businesses that were hit. Find out who the investigating officers were and whether they have any other information that might help us. Actually, better call the Edmonton police about the other two while you're at it."

Friday, December 7

By the next morning, I had news from the forensic lab in Regina. The latest bomb had been live and a discussion with Dr. McDecy in Ottawa had produced the conclusion that it was of the exact same type and construction as the Ontario bombs and, being so new and unique, almost certainly made by the same person. Julie had news too.

"I found out that the Hamilton Police investigated the one Ontario break-in, and Nepean Police[35] the second," she said. "In each case I talked to the actual investigators, but they had nothing to go on so far. No fingerprints, no witnesses, and neither company had security cameras so no tapes or photos. They didn't say it in so many words, but the message each one gave me was that they'd already done more than was warranted by two small, low priority thefts and they weren't planning to do anything more unless fresh evidence shows up.

"I next called the Edmonton police and tracked down the investigating officers there too. Same thing in both cases, no evidence, no witnesses, and no further action as they weren't high-priority cases for them either. Sorry."

"Well, that's how it goes," I replied. "The timing, locations, and specific things taken make me think it was the work of our bomber, but they're obviously not stupid or careless. We may have to just stay on the trail until they make a mistake."

"What's next then?"

"I think we've done all we can do from here. Let's get on up to Edmonton, collect our vehicles – I'd like to see if we can scare-up some portable radios, maps, and field-glasses too – and continue on from there. I think we should visit the two Edmonton area break-in sites ourselves, and then the pipeline company's head of security is going to give us a tour of a pump station."

Julie had originally hitched a ride with a colleague to get to Innisfail, so I offered her and Scout a ride to Edmonton with Silver and I. I still had my red crew-cab pickup truck, so there was lots of room for Julie and I in front and the two dogs in the back seat (in perfect symmetry during the lower-speed portions of the journey, were Silver sticking his head out of one side window and Scout the other). It was only a two-hour drive, so it was mid-morning when we pulled into the parking lot of the RCMP's K Division headquarters building. The staff at the main desk were aware of the provision of vehicles being made for us and a corporal showed us to the vehicles, which were a pair of large, unmarked, black SUVs. The corporal explained that they were normally used by VIP security details and were fully equipped with radios, sirens, and inconspicuous emergency lights (inconspicuous until they were turned-on, that is).

Julie asked whether we could borrow two hand-held radios as well and, after a bit of searching around on the corporal's part, we were finally issued with two Motorola MX300 hand-held VHF radios that had crystals for the standard and tactical frequencies, just like the SUVs, so we would be able to use them portable-to-portable or portable-to-vehicle.

"These are very similar to the models we used in Alaska two years ago[36]," said Julie, looking them over.

The corporal was unsuccessful at finding field-glasses we could borrow, but I wasn't worried about that as they would be easy enough for us to purchase on our own. He did, however, arrange for me to be able to store my own truck in the police vehicle compound, which was probably the most secure place in the whole city I could have stored it.

After we'd transferred our gear into the police vehicles and parked my own truck, we found places to stop and buy field-glasses, and lunch, and then finally drove to Spruce Grove, which was only a 20-minute drive west of Edmonton's city limits.

We interviewed the agrochemical supplier's store manager but didn't learn much. Someone had broken in late at night, helped themselves to 3 kg of ammonium nitrate, and then left without leaving any traces except small puddles of water from the intruder's boots and a set of slightly windswept holes in the snow outside that suggested very large winter boots of some kind. The intruder had walked along the front street for some time before entering the grounds of the store, thus leaving no trail for anyone to follow. The manager explained that the cash register had been emptied that day, with the cash drawer left open so no one would bother to break into the machine.

"Do you have a security system installed?" asked Julie.

"Yes," replied the manager, with a sigh. "And it's the latest thing too. The door and window sensors are attached to a mechanical phone-dialing system that sends a pre-recorded alert message to the security company, who are supposed to call the police first and then me."

"What happened?" I asked.

"Our thief was too smart for us. They found the telephone wire where it comes into the building and cut it, so when the sensor switch closed at the window they broke into, the machine did the dialing and played the tape, but no signal got out. All that money spent for nothing," he complained.

"That wasn't very helpful," said Julie, after we'd thanks the manager and walked over to our vehicles.

"No," I agreed. "Let's try the electroplating company next. It's more or less on our way back downtown anyway."

The Edmonton metal plating and finishing that had been hit was in the north, industrial part of Edmonton and didn't look very promising from the outside. It was on a back street, among a row of rough-looking buildings, each of which had a small parking lot to one side, and bit of a back lot filled with various crates and what looked like scrap metal. The back lots were encircled by steel fencing topped with coils of barbed-wire. To complete the picture, the shop we were headed for had an older model pickup truck parked out front that looked like it might have been made in the 1960s and had taken a lot of abuse over the years.

"I bet we'd have a field-day with that truck if we were here on traffic duty," said Julie, as we emerged from our own vehicles, which we'd parked right behind it.

"I don't think I'd take that bet," I said, looking at the rear brake, signal, and licence plate lights and wondering what the odds were that any of them were operable.

When we entered the shop, the single employee was engaged with a huge man – he was easily over six feet tall and built like a football linebacker - wearing heavy leather boots, faded jeans, an army-surplus winter parka, and a blue bandanna tied around a thick mop of dark, uncombed hair.

"I don't care what it costs, I want this done right and if it ain't, I'll come back and torch this whole place. You got that?" he was saying to the man behind the counter.

"Don't you worry sir. I've been in this business a long time and I know what I'm doing. You come back next week and I'll have this chromed up so nicely you'll want to use it as a shaving mirror."

"Well, you'd better," the man growled ungraciously as he turned to walk away. When he saw Julie and I, both in tactical uniforms and accompanied by Silver and Scout, he did a double-take. For a moment, I thought he was going to make some kind of smart remark. He paused, then obviously thought better of it, set his jaw, stomped out without saying another word, and slammed the door behind him.

With the sound of slamming door still echoing in our ears, Julie said, "Are all your customers like him?"

"Well, yes, actually quite a few of them are," said the man behind the counter. "You see a lot of our business involves cleaning and chrome-plating the metal parts of motorcycles, especially the big machines like Harleys that the bikers have. You know, if they can find the money, they'll get every bit of exposed metal chromed if they can? Anyway, the tough-guy persona is a cultural thing with them. They all have to appear tough and mean or angry. Some of them really are. For most of them its just an act, but you can't call them on it or they'll have to follow-through. If you go along with it, then they're pretty easy to get along with."

"I can see that you know your business," I said.

"Well, I own it, so I should. Like you probably heard me tell our young, angry friend just now, I've been in this business a long time. If you survive, you learn a few things."

"You mean, if you learn a few things, you survive."

"Heh, heh. Yup, that's it exactly. Now then, what can I do for you officers?"

"We'd like to ask you a few questions, if you don't mind, about the break-in you had about a week ago."

"The break-in? Oh that! That was a strange one alright. Didn't take much, just some perchloric acid from the back and nearly five-hundred bucks that my idiot of an apprentice had left in the till. I wasn't feeling well and had gone home early, leaving him to close-up. Damn fool."

It wasn't clear whether his last remark was directed at the apprentice or himself, but I left it alone. "We were wondering whether there is anything else you might be able to tell us."

"Well, it was strange, that's for sure. He could have taken away a small fortune in expensive metals, or any of the chromed parts that were finished and waiting for customers to pick them up, but instead he only takes a jug of acid and some cash. What kind of idiot does that?"

"Maybe a very focused one," I said. "You said 'he.' What makes you think it was a man?"

"Oh, he walked like a man. You could see it plain as day on the security tape." He stepped back and pointed up and to one side where we could just make out the face of a camera lens hidden in among the leaves of a large plastic plant that was mounted high on a corner shelf.

"Security tape? The Edmonton police didn't say anything about a security tape!" said Julie.

"Well, they didn't ask me, did they? Came in, took a quick look around, made a few notes and left. Acted like a little business like mine wasn't worth their time. Like I was inconveniencing them. So, I was just as happy to see them get out as they were to leave." I noticed that his entire manner had changed from ingratiating to irritated and scornful.

"We're sorry you were treated that way. That's not fair. We'd like to know more though. Do you still have the tape?"

"I think so. Come on to the back and I'll check." As he led us out of the front office and into the back we entered a very factory-like shop. It was almost like following an assembly line as he showed us where metal pieces would come in, get cleaned, have parts ground off or welded onto them, followed by one or more electroplating baths, then final polishing, and in some cases have a clear protective coating sprayed on. Off in a corner was a small office in which he had a VHS videocassette recorder and a small TV monitor.

"I wired-up a switch, because the machine can only record four hours on a tape" he explained. "Anytime the cash register drawer gets opened, the switch closes, which turns the camera on and starts the recorder taping. When the drawer closes, everything turns off. That way the tape lasts all day and if there's ever a holdup or a break-in, the register drawer gets left open and the system records until the drawer is closed or the tape runs out. When we had the robbery, the recorder came on when thief opened the register drawer. Here's the tape."

After he'd inserted the tape and made sure it was rewound, he hit play and we watched. At first the image was just grey and fuzzy as the black-and-white video camera came on and warmed up. When an image bloomed into focus, we could see someone standing in front of the cash register, removing the cash. It certainly looked like a man, of medium height. After that, he adjusted his grip on something he was carrying under his left arm, presumably the stolen perchloric acid. Then, without turning around he walked around the front counter, crossed to the front door, and left.

"Too bad he didn't turn to face the camera," the owner said.

"Yes, but you're right that it looks like a man, and we now have an idea of his height at least. Do you think we could borrow this tape and have our forensic people look at it?" I asked.

"You can keep it. But why are you Mounties interested in a break-in that even the local cops don't think is worth investigating?"

"It's not the break-in we're interested in, it's what he stole."

"The perchloric… wait a minute, you're worried someone's going to make a bomb, right?"

"Let's just say that if someone out there wants to make a bomb then we want to stop them. You can help us, too." I handed him a card with a toll-free phone number on it. "If you hear about any more perchloric or perchlorate thefts, would you please leave me a message at this number?"

"Wow. OK, sure." He looked at me for a moment. "I'll call if I ever hear about any nitrate thefts too, like from a fertilizer dealer for example?"

"It's always nice meeting a quick-thinker," I said, with a smile. "Thank you for all your help."

"What do you think Julie?" I asked, when we were outside, walking toward our vehicles.

"Looked like a male, medium height, average build, hair cut short, and he was bent-over just a bit when he walked," said Julie.

"Agreed. It's not much, but we're starting to get a profile on him. I doubt that the forensic lab will catch anything we didn't but we'll send it in just in case."

The next day, we drove to the pipeline company's Stony Plain pump station, which was very close to Spruce Grove, where we'd just been the previous day.

Ed Williams was waiting for us when we drove up, and he unlocked the fence gate and waved us through. As we waited, he got into his own vehicle and led us deeper into the compound. As we drove, we could see that there was a large, light green shed with pipes leading into and out of it, some smaller sheds, a small maze of pipes and valves connecting this way and that, and another structure that was more like a light green roof on stilts. Under the roof, we could see the place where the main pipeline rose up out of the ground, and another where it dipped back down underground.

"Thanks for coming out on a Sunday to help us, Ed. We appreciate it," I began, when we'd exited our vehicles.

"You're very welcome. The feeling's mutual, and our company's executives are pleased that you're taking this seriously."

"Well, our bomber has already derailed a train causing a massive fire, a lot of destruction, some injuries, and one death, so there's no doubt it's serious."

"No ransom demands then?" asked Ed.

"I was about to ask you the same question. In the rail incident, no, there was no early warning and no ransom demand. I'm not sure he wanted to kill anyone either. He could just as easily have derailed a passenger train and killed hundreds, but he chose a freight train."

"More like making a statement then?"

"Seems like it. We've received three letters so far, all of them constructed the same way. One of them came with a bomb that he didn't even try to detonate, and in it, he basically challenged us to try to catch him."

"So. Someone with a grudge then," Ed mused.

"Maybe. We don't know much yet."

Shrugging his shoulders, Ed got down to the business at hand and gave us a tour of the site which, being fairly small, didn't take long. Basically, the main pipeline came up out of the ground, went through a battery of pipes and valves and pumps that collectively boosted the internal pressure, after which the pipeline went back underground and from there on to the next pump station.

"Do they all look like this?" I asked him.

"Pretty much. The pumps, connections, valves, and controls are all standard. There are a few variations in the layout depending on the local terrain, such as if the ground is particularly rocky, or sloped, like when it's running through the mountains."

"OK then. If you were a bomber, where would you strike?"

"I'm way ahead of you on that one. I asked our chief engineer the same question. He says that if you want to shut down operations for the maximum time possible, then you hit the pumps. If you do, you could damage or destroy most of them in a single strike, not to mention damaging the valves and controls. It would take time to get the replacements and to rebuild the infrastructure. If, on the other hand, you just want to make a public statement, then he says you hit the main pipeline on the high-pressure side of the system, just before it goes back underground. If you're lucky, and you detonate it when there's a batch of refined oil or other refined oil product going through, then you hit the jackpot and you'll get a huge concussive blast, a big fireball, and maximum heat wave radiating out. If not, and it's crude oil going through, then you'll still get an explosion, lots of fire, and a plume of smoke that can be seen for miles."

"Not good either way," I observed.

"Not good at all."

"Are all the sites this exposed?" I asked, looking beyond the fence to the expanse of prairie that extended out in all directions around us. Here and there, the landscape was decorated with clumps of very tall trees or rows of shorter trees, but not much else. The former were probably original, natural-growth trees, I thought, while the latter had clearly been planted to serve as windbreaks – a common practice of farmers on the prairies. *Lots of places to hide a sniper,* I thought.

"Most of them are like this, yes, although a few in the mountains are just a patch carved out of the forest."

"Do you mind if we let the dogs sniff around?" I asked.

"No. Not at all. You don't think…."

"I don't think there's likely to be a bomb here right now, no, but it won't hurt to let the dogs get familiar with the layout." I motioned to Julie and we each let our dog off-leash with orders to search.

Silver and Scout sprang into action, and we just stood where we were and chatted about inconsequential things while we watched and waited as the dogs did their thing. We lost sight of them as they worked their way around in the maze of pipes and valves and things, and after a while it seemed like things had become very quiet.

As the silence became uncomfortable, Julie eventually said "Alex...."

"Silver!" I called out, and was rewarded with a muffled "*Grruph*" that seemed to come from the far side of the compound.

The three of us jogged over towards the sound, and as we rounded a bunch of above-ground pipes and valves, we could see Silver and Scout sitting patiently on their haunches, near the roofed structure that contained a bunch of machinery and from which the main pipeline exited before angling down towards the ground. As we took a few steps closer, I suddenly stopped and raised an arm to signal a halt.

Damn!

"Do you see that little circle of bright orange about a foot off the ground on the side of that machinery?" I asked.

"My God! It's another one," gasped Julie.

"Go call this in and ask for the Edmonton bomb squad, would you please?" The words were no sooner out of my mouth, than Julie had called for Scout to join her and ran towards her SUV where she could get on the radio.

"Would you mind backing up a bit and waiting while I go take a look?" I asked Ed.

"Sure, whatever you say," he replied. He wasn't being cowardly; he was being sensible. He knew very well that if the bomb was detonated, he could do more good if he was still alive and functioning than otherwise.

I looked around. The bomber, if he was even out there watching, could be hiding on any of several dozen places, and could easily be long gone before we could organize enough help to do a ground and air search.

I still didn't know what our bomber was up to, but I didn't think he was trying to kill people. At least I hoped not, as I walked up to where Silver was still patiently waiting.

"Good boy Silver. Well done," I said, stroking his fur while I took a closer look at the orange circle. It was on the cap of one of two bottles, jammed side by side into some machinery that was attached to the main pipeline, just before it exited the shelter. It looked exactly like the one from Innisfail, and exactly like the unexploded one from Ontario.

Telling Silver to stay put, I slowly walked up to the bright orange disk. It still looked exactly like the previous bombs. I turned 180 degrees and scanned the horizon looking for places a shooter could hide. *Useless.* There were plenty of stands of trees and undergrowth with a clear line of sight to where I was.

I turned back to the bomb and took a closer look this time. About an inch away from the bomb, something caught my eye. An envelope had been wedged in to the machinery too.

Well, I'll be damned, I thought, *another letter!*

Reaching out, I carefully removed the envelope. There were no wires or anything, attaching it to the bomb, it was a message, not a trigger. I stood up and walked away, collecting Silver as I went. As I approached Ed, I simply waved the envelope at him and kept on walking.

"This is your lucky day, I think. He's not going to blow up your station, he's delivering another message, just for us. Let's go open it."

Despite my brave words, I waited until we were at the vehicles with Julie and Scout, and well away from the bomb before opening the letter. Handling it carefully, so as not to smudge any fingerprints or important markings (not that I thought there would be any) I used my knife to slit the envelope open and extract the letter. "Letters cut from magazine covers and pasted onto plain paper, just like the others," I said to Ed, showing it to him and Julie. The letter read: "COULD HAVE KILLED YOU – DIDN'T."

I found out later that the letters were from the covers of Macleans magazines published during the same period as before, between August and December of the previous year.

Laurie Schramm

5 WILD GOOSE CHASE

Having found the bomb – just one – and the note, Julie and I positioned our SUVs at the junction between the highway and the connecting road to the pump station and, with emergency lights flashing, had stopped and directed traffic as necessary to keep people away from the station while we waited for the Edmonton Police Service's bomb squad to come deal with the device. Via the radio room at Edmonton HQ, I'd sent a message to my boss, Bob, in Ottawa with the by now usual request that he arrange for the bomb squad not to detonate the bomb until we'd had a forensic explosives expert look it over. There seemed little doubt, however, that it was made by the bomber we were after.

While we waited, I had lots of time to think, but it didn't help.

So many riddles.

We didn't know what the bomber was going to do next, or where, or why, nor even whether there was still an outstanding threat to the pipeline or not.

Once we finally got back to the Edmonton hotel room Julie and I were sharing, I called Bob directly to discuss the latest developments. We both thought that the bomber had already accomplished his immediate purpose, in showing his power over us. He could have blown up the line but he chose not to. He could have shot any of Julie, Ed, Silver, Scout or me – I had no doubts about his marksmanship – but he chose not to. On the other hand, Bob agreed with me that we couldn't afford to take the risk that there would be no more strikes against the pipeline. That meant we had to check the rest of the line as far as Jasper.

Ed was pleased by our decision to put the safety of 'his' pipeline first and was very accommodating when we asked for maps and locations of the rest of the pump stations and the few places where, for other reasons, the pipeline rose up and ran above ground for reasonably short distances. It was also agreed that we would keep him advised of our progress and that he would have someone meet us at each pump station to unlock the gates and provide any other help we might need.

The next morning, on Bob's advice, we returned to K Division HQ to be issued with carbine rifles, for which Bob had already managed to gain authorization from higher ups in the chain of command. From there, we went and picked up Ed's maps from the pipeline's Edmonton office, and then to the Yellowhead Highway to drive to the next station, which was at Gainford.

I'd decided that Julie and I would do the searches together as it was safer for us to have a human partner, and it was much faster having two sniffing dogs at a time do the searching. It took us an hour to get to the Gainford station and an hour to search it. That brought the morning to a close, and we stopped for lunch at the next promising-looking highway-side restaurant. One benefit of being in uniform and on duty was that we could bring the dogs into restaurants with us rather than having to look for places with outside seating, which is what I normally did when working undercover (weather permitting).

In the afternoon, we conducted searches at the Chip, Wolf, and Edson stations after which it was time to give the dogs a break, so we checked into a motel in Edson. That was nice, because we could clearly see the Rocky Mountains in the distance and smell the mountain air courtesy of the westerly winds.

The next day, we worked our way to Jasper, stopping at the Hinton station, a couple places where the pipeline rose up and ran on low trestles that rose about 1 metre (3 ft) above ground for a stretch, and finally the Jasper station. That took all day, but it did give us an excuse to rent a small cottage on the outskirts of town for the night, which was beautiful. Unfortunately, the lovely scenery and fresh mountain air didn't make up for the fact that we'd just spent a tiring two days of searching without result.

Ed, at the pipeline company, received our empty search results as very good news, however, and promised to keep extra security patrols in place and remain vigilant for at least another week or two.

When I phoned Bob, in Ottawa, he sounded as frustrated as I was with the wild-goose chases we'd been on. Following our discussion, he agreed with me that we might as well head back to Edmonton and wait there for a while, pending another development in the case, whether good or bad.

The next day, we drove back to Edmonton. Without having to stop for searches, but making one stop for lunch, it took us nearly five hours. Plenty of time for me to think.

On the one hand, we had a good team. In addition to the real searches, I'd arranged for us to occasionally lay practice scent-trails, with one of us planting a dummy bomb containing real explosive but no detonator. As we'd conducted search after search, both real and practice, Julie and Scout had each watched Silver and I working together and made adjustments to their own methods. Julie, for example, became less directive and increasingly let Scout find his own way. Scout, for his part, seemed to adopt some of Silver's searching tactics while still maintaining his own personal style.

By the time we'd conducted twelve real and practice searches, over several days, Julie and Scout's performance as a team was much improved, and Scout's searching had become very nearly as efficient and effective as Silver's. Julie, for her part, had been concentrating so hard on the tasks at hand that she hadn't noticed the improvement, so when I pointed this out and praised her work, she was quite surprised, and pleased.

I had fully expected to be able to work seamlessly with Julie because we'd worked so well together in Alaska two years earlier, but now we had an effective team of four.

On the other hand, I wished that I could figure out how to make better use of our capabilities. We knew that the bomber was male, of medium height and build, and was quite cunning. He'd been very careful thus far, but had made at least two mistakes already, in that he was repeating the same methods to get his chemicals, and he hadn't spotted the security camera at the metal - plating shop in Edmonton. Other than that, he remained a step or more ahead of us at every turn, and his motivations and goals remained a mystery.

Obviously, he was playing some kind of elaborate cat-and-mouse game with us, making it serious enough to hold our attention by planting real bombs in places he could easily have simply placed empty bottles with bright orange caps.

I doubted that he was actually following us as we danced to his tune, but I wouldn't have put it past him to have been observing us – from a safe distance – at the Innisfail and Stony Plain bomb placements. That would have allowed him to make sure we were following his bread-crumbs, given him the pleasure of knowing he could have detonated the bombs if he'd wanted to (the Stony Plain one, at least, was in a very exposed location), and he would now know who was on his trail – Julie and I – and what we and our vehicles looked like.

I'd like to have a crystal ball to tell me what he's planning now, and what his end-game is, I thought.

When we reached Edmonton, we checked-in at the RCMP's K Division headquarters building once more, and I was pleased to learn that a set of large prints from the aerial photos was ready for us to pick up. What surprised me, was that they came in two large, and rather heavy, boxes. I had expected something more like a thick folder, but when I examined the boxes, I found out how naive I'd been.

Included in the first box was a set of typed notes describing the dates and times of the flights, comments on weather and visibility, and an index to the various numbered prints. The photographer had used a professional, medium-format, SLR (single-lens-reflex) camera loaded with double-length 220 roll-film, on which the camera recorded 6 x 4.5 cm format images. That meant negative images that were three times larger than those of standard 35 mm film, and up to 30 frames per roll.

A sketch-map was also included, showing that for each flight mission the aircraft had flown in two broad arcs, rather than straight lines. In addition, the arcs were opposing, meaning that each arc curved slightly, around the pump station, and from different sides. Bob must have either been very persuasive or had convinced a higher authority to back us up, because the first flight mission took place on the very evening of the day in which I had made the request, then there were four more flown on each of the next two days, plus a single morning flight on the day following the one in which we found the bomb. That meant ten flights were flown. For each flight, there were two arcs flown, with a full roll of film being shot along each arc. Obviously, after the first arc, the photographer changed the film while the aircraft was looping around for the second pass. Altogether that produced nearly 620 12 x 18-inch prints, which filled most of the two boxes.

No wonder my request had given Bob pause!

Finally, whomever had put everything together for us had even foreseen the possibility that we would need a magnifying glass, as they had included two magnifying lenses, one with a handle for rapid scanning of the prints and another, more powerful, lens that was mounted on a small stand.

Making a mental note to remember to thank the Air Services people for everything, Julie and I carted the boxes out to our vehicles and headed for our hotel. We had a lot of work cut out for us now, and along the way we stopped at a photographic supply store to buy a second set of magnifiers and a couple of lamps for extra illumination.

The next two days were spent poring through the aerial photos.

The first thing we noticed was how sharp the images were. The pump station compound stood out very clearly, as did the nearby clumps and rows of trees, plus several of the nearby range roads. Within the compound, we could make out the individual pumps and the types of parked vehicles, but not such fine details as specific vehicle models or licence plates. This was encouraging.

At first, it was fun looking at the images to see what we could discern. Later, it just became tedious working through photo after photo. By the end of the day, we'd looked at all 620, but they were all beginning to look the same to us, so I called a halt.

To give ourselves a break, we brought in take-out food and ate in front of a movie in my hotel room, after which we turned-in early for the night. I hoped that a good night's sleep would give us clear minds in the morning.

Maybe it was the rest, or maybe it was simply granting our subconscious minds time to process everything we'd looked at. Whatever it was, when we went back to the photos after breakfast the next day, things began to jump out at us.

It was Julie who first noticed that, while some vehicles appeared and then disappeared at various times and places, there was one vehicle that appeared numerous times in the same location, well outside the pump station compound.

It hadn't been easy to spot in the first place, because it was parked in a clump of trees and brush beside one of the range roads. The fact that it was parked nose-in between two trees meant that it was only visible in the photos from one of the arcs flown on each sortie, not both. Once we knew what to look for, however, it was easy to locate in several other photos.

"It's here on all four sorties flown on December 7th, and again for all four sorties flown on the 8th, but only for the two morning sorties flown on the 9th," said Julie excitedly, "and I can't find it anywhere on the 10th."

"Here it is on the evening of the 6th," I said, looking up from one of the prints, "but in a different location! This time it's parked close to the pump station fence.

"So," I summarized, "suppose our bomber parked near the pump station on the evening of the 6th so he could plant the bomb and the letter. Having it close at hand would mean he could get away fast, and he would have thought it unlikely that we'd be there that soon to begin searching."

"OK."

"For the next few days, it's parked further away, partially hidden beside a range road. Our bomber could have positioned himself in that very same clump of trees, or even in one of the nearby ones, to watch for us. In that case, if he needed to get away quickly, such as if he saw us organizing a ground search outside the compound, he'd have been able to quickly get to one of several intersections with other range roads giving him multiple getaway routes.

"Now, on the morning of the 9th, he's there to see us arrive, search the compound and find the bomb and the letter. That's success for him. He probably stays put until he sees us leave, then he gets into his vehicle and drives off, never to return."

"Perfect!" said Julie, excitedly clapping her hands.

"I think it's pretty likely that's what happened. Now, the photos where you found the vehicle suggest a dark-coloured pickup truck with a white cap on the back, or possibly a full-size SUV in two-tone colours. Right?"

"Yes, but it looks more like a cap on a truck box at the back because of the slope of the cap's sides and it almost looks like the cap sticks out just a bit at the bottom on each side," added Julie.

"OK, I agree, but we'll keep the SUV option in mind just in

case, I think. Now then, on the evening of the 6th, the vehicle is parked out in the open near the compound. Julie, can you find the photo from the same evening that has a similar view but from the other arc that the plane would have flown?"

It took a few moments for her to sort through the stacks of photos, but she was ultimately successful. Knowing exactly where to look, she soon found it. "Here it is" she said, triumphantly. In one image, the vehicle was partially obscured by the fencing, but the other view was clear, and showed the vehicle from its side.

"Definitely a pickup truck, not an SUV," I said, peering at the image with our most powerful magnifying glass. "The truck body seems to be flat black, or at least extremely dark, and the cap on the back is definitely white. What do you think?"

"Flat black body, with a white cap," said Julie, sounding very definite.

"That matches the security video from the Edmonton heist, which showed a dark-coloured, older model pickup truck," I added, "so that gives me a bit more confidence that we're on to something here.

"Now let's go back to all the shots from the other days that show the truck parked between the trees off the range road. We're looking to see if one of them shows the rear licence plate."

We only found one photo in which the licence plate was visible. The bomber mustn't have parked so deeply into the brush in that one, because the truck was actually angled nose down, giving the photographer a clear shot of the plate.

"White background," I murmured, straining to make out details through the magnifying glass. "That eliminates the ones with coloured backgrounds[37]: BC, Alberta, Manitoba, PEI, and Newfoundland. The letters seem to be dark blue or black. That eliminates Saskatchewan, New Brunswick, and the Yukon."

"It's rectangular though, right?" asked Julie. "That would eliminate the Northwest Territories, which have polar-bear-shaped plates."

"That's right. Good point Julie. So that leaves us with Ontario, Quebec, and Nova Scotia. Ontario, I know, uses three letters then a crown then three numbers, but Quebec uses three numbers, a letter, then another three numbers. I don't remember what Nova Scotia's look like, do you?"

Julie didn't, but a few phone calls produced the answer that it was three pairs of numbers separated by dots. We couldn't tell for sure, but Julie and I agreed that the licence plate most looked like Ontario's.

"So, there we have it Julie," I concluded. "A dark-coloured pickup truck painted flat black or something similarly dark, with a white cap on the box, and probably bearing Ontario plates, but possibly Quebec or Nova Scotia."

"Right," said Julie, "and if we combine the suspect descriptions from the Ontario rail bombing and the Edmonton store break-in, we get a probable description of the bomber as a mature adult male, medium height and slender build, probably fair-skinned, with thin, fairly straight, greying hair, possibly parted near the middle, possibly prone to walk with a bit of a stoop. Last seen wearing a dark hoodie."

"It's still going to be like looking for a needle in a haystack, I'm afraid...."

Julie noticed that I'd ended up staring off into space. "What are you thinking?" she asked.

"I was thinking that we know one more thing. We know of a single location that he visited several days in a row. I wonder how careful he was about not leaving traces behind."

"You mean the place he used to watch for us at the Spruce Grove pump station."

"Yes. I can't think of anything better for us to do right now than drive out there tomorrow and take a look."

The next morning was a chilly -5 °C (23 °F), but at least the sky was clear and the sun was shining as we drove back out to Spruce Grove. With the aid of a map and our aerial photos, it was easy to find the clump of trees and bushes, and even the exact spot at which the black and white truck had been parked. Although it had been six days since the bomber had last parked his truck there, only a light snow had fallen, not enough to fully obscure the deep tire tracks where he'd driven off the range road, nor the bent and broken bushes where he'd driven the nose of the truck in.

Julie and I had no sooner finished looking at the tire tracks and the adjacent bushes, than the two dogs had discovered the observation spot. There, nestled in among the trees, was a blanket-covered groundsheet, frozen to the ground.

"It must have gotten wet, with all his comings and goings," I mused, "and then frozen in place."

"Must have thought it was too much work to pry out, especially since he didn't need it any more," said Julie.

"Yes. He must have thought that we either wouldn't have guessed he'd be watching, or else that we wouldn't waste time searching for his observation point. Careless of him…. What is it Silver?"

My thoughts had been interrupted by Silver growling while scratching and sniffing at the blanket. I tried asking him again, while looking directly into his eyes. "He's unhappy with the scent for some reason, but I have no idea why. Let's look around and see if he left anything else behind."

Each of us taking one side, we searched the surrounding bushes on hands and knees which, since everything was covered in snow, quickly left us wet and cold, but we did find lots of cigarette butts and a few other things. Julie found a white sheet, presumably used for camouflage, that had been loosely rolled up and tossed away. On my side, I found a few plastic bags that seemed to contain wrappings of the kind that were commonly used to package sandwiches in vending machines.

"Not bad," I concluded, as Julie and I stood up to stretch our backs and wipe away some of the snow and dirt we'd accumulated. "Let's take the garbage back to the Ident[38] people and ask them to look for prints, and we should keep the sheet and the blanket so we have a scent source for Silver and Scout if we ever need it."

We had brought some large-sized garbage bags with us, which was used for the items we found. Then, before we left, I took a pair of field glasses from my truck and went back to the bomber's observation point. Kneeling low on the spot that had formerly held the groundsheet, I used the field glasses to look out at the pump station. *Hmmm*, I thought.

"Well, Julie. He certainly picked a good spot. He'd have seen everything we did, and he even had a clear view of the place where he stuck the bomb and the letter."

"I still can't figure out why he would be going to all this time and trouble. If he's making and placing all these bombs, why not detonate more of them?"

"Yes, the more this goes on, the more it looks like he's mainly just trying to lead us around by the nose. So, will he get tired of it after a while, or is it all leading somewhere?"

The following day, we went to K-Division HQ in Edmonton and dropped off the bag full of the bomber's garbage with a request for a fingerprint check.

Then, while I went to talk to the photographic people about the possibility of further enlarging the best aerial photos of the suspect truck, I sent Julie to contact CPIC to find out whether there were any new break-in reports that might be of interest to us.

I struck out with my task. Although the Ident people were very obliging, further enlargement of the aerial photos we'd selected produced prints that were too grainy to show any additional detail.

Julie, on the other hand, came back with some 'probables.' There had been two more break-and-enter thefts of interest to us. Both of them were recent, and both in the same community: Grande Prairie, a modest-size city in northwest Alberta. One was an agrochemical supplier and the other a metal-plating and polishing business.

"That certainly sounds like our bomber," I said. "If so, he's getting repetitive. I think we should go there and talk to them."

It was afternoon already, and we'd just paused for coffee and a chat with colleagues when a constable came in from the radio room with a fax that had arrived for us. This was a bit of a novelty, because fax machines had only recently[39] began replacing telex machines for urgent, printed messages.

It was letter #5, and it read: "BAD NEWS FOR A BC GAS WELL."

"A gas well in BC," said Julie. "That's not very specific. How many of them do you think there are?"

"I don't know. Less than there are in Alberta though. I guess we'll have to find out."

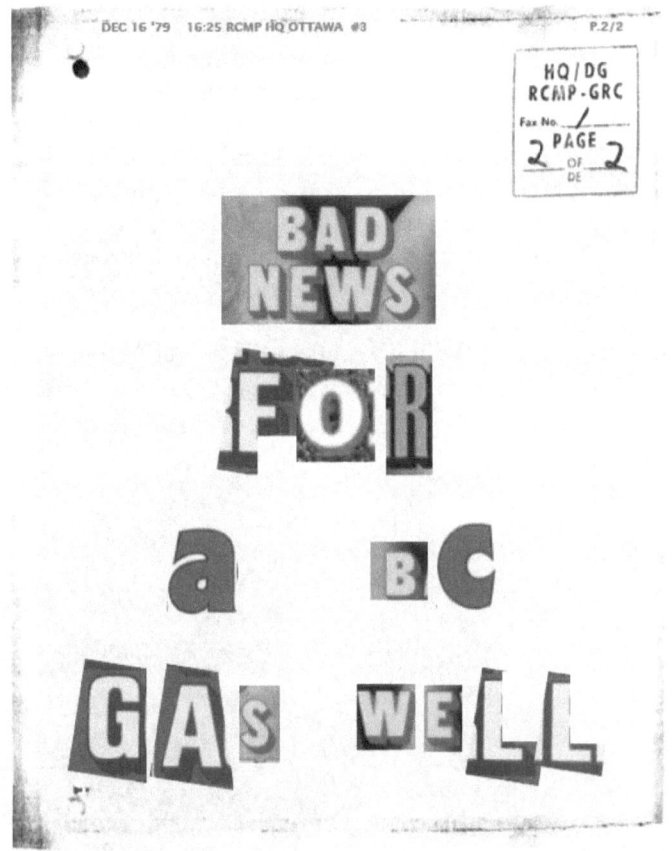

An hour of phone calls later and we had some information, at least. Julie took a stab at summarizing what we'd learned: "OK. All of the commercial oil and gas production is in BC's northeast. That helps a bit. Most of the wells seem to have been drilled within the past five years, and they are in what's called the 'Deep Basin' region south of Dawson Creek. The total number of oil and gas wells in the province is just over 600, although some are inactive and others are incomplete[40]. In the past year alone, 175 new wells were drilled, of which 86 are potential gas producers[41]."

"Whew!" I exclaimed. "That's too many wells to watch all at once. It's like the pipeline problem all over again. At least Ottawa will notify the BC government and the individual well drillers and operators of the threat.

"On the other hand, Grande Prairie is on the way to Dawson Creek, so let's head that way tomorrow. We can check out the break-ins for ourselves and then head for the general area of the wells, at least. The other thing we can do, is to have an alert sent to the detachments in the vicinity of Grande Prairie and Dawson Creek, asking them to be on the alert for a black pickup truck with a white cap, probably bearing Ontario, Quebec, or Nova Scotia plates. We'll list it observe and report, but do not approach; suspect is considered armed and dangerous."

"So, we go back on the road again."

"Yes. Tomorrow. We'll cover Grande Prairie first and then if nothing else comes up we'll take a look at the Dawson Creek area."

6 ANOTHER STRIKE

December 17, 1979
Grande Prairie, Alberta

With a stop for coffee (and a stretch for the dogs) along the way, it took us just over five hours to drive to Grande Prairie. It was actually a pretty nice drive as we had good winter driving conditions on the highway and, along the way, I enjoyed watching the emergence of the Rocky Mountains in the distance.

Grande Prairie is policed by a detachment of the RCMP so, following a quick lunch, we dropped in there partly as a courtesy call and partly so we could read the police reports on the two break-ins. They were brief and to the point, and didn't provide us with much in the way of new information. We spent the rest of the afternoon visiting the two break-in sites.

The break-in at the agrochemical supplier seemed to have been very similar to the one we investigated in Spruce Grove. Once again, someone had broken in late at night, helped themselves to a large bag of ammonium nitrate, and left. In this case, the burglar had climbed an access ladder at the back of an adjacent building, crossed from one roof to the next, and then broke in through a plexiglass skylight window. From the skylight, the burglar was able to jump to the top of a tall set of shelves and then climb down, leaving behind tracks in the snow on the roof – large winter boot tracks again – and a variety of items scattered on the floor that had been dislodged while climbing down. All of these things the manager showed us in the form of photographs taken the next morning as, since then, the skylight had been covered over, the mess cleaned up, and another snowfall had covered the original tracks.

According to the manager, no cash was stolen because the cash registers had been emptied out when the store closed for the day.

"Do you have a security system?" I asked.

"Yes," replied the manager, "but only with magnetic-switch sensors on the windows and doors. It seems that, when it was installed, no one thought about the roof. Of course, now that we've learned our lesson, we're having a sensor installed when they come to replace the skylight. Fortunately, we only lost the one bag of fertilizer and the broken skylight, so it was probably a pretty cheap lesson for us," he added ruefully.

"How did the burglar get out?" asked Julie.

"Switched off the security system from the inside, then unlocked one of the back doors and walked out. Pretty simple, when you come to think about it."

"No closed-circuit video?" asked Julie.

"No. But we're considering adding a system for the future."

"Did anyone see anything suspicious, or even anything out of the ordinary?" I asked.

"No. The local police asked us that too, when they were here, but the first we learned of the break-in was when I came to open the store the next morning. When we looked around the back, there was just a set of boot-prints in the snow leading across the parking lot to the back alley, but by that time there had been enough vehicle and foot traffic to cover the trail so we don't even know which direction the tracks went."

That seemed to be everything. Consistent with the Spruce Grove break-in, but no new clues beyond a reaffirmation that our bomber was fairly bright.

We visited the metal-plating and polishing company next. In contrast to the Edmonton shop, this one was more modern-looking, and was bright and clean inside. Business, at this place, was obviously good. The manager was a young man of about 25.

We introduced ourselves, and explained that we wanted to ask him a few questions about his recent break-in.

"There isn't much to tell. Someone broke in during the night and stole a few things. Not much, really, some perchloric acid, a few tools, and some plastic bottles."

"What kind of plastic bottles?" I asked.

"Oh. Nalgene®[42]. The one-litre, wide-mouth kind. I use them for mixing and storing small batches of chemicals, and I even sell some to local hikers and campers. They like them because you can store cold or hot liquids in them and they won't leak in a backpack."

"I know," I smiled. "I have a few of them myself for the same reason."

"It was such an odd mixture of things that I first thought that maybe someone just broke-in, grabbed a few things at random and then bolted."

"But now?" I prompted.

"When I heard about the fertilizer theft, I put two and two together. Now, seeing you two show-up here, I guess you're thinking the same thing."

"Yes. With a little knowledge, and both of the stolen chemicals, someone could make the essentials of a simple explosive. And those stolen bottles are made of high-density polyethylene. With a little care and the right technique, they'd make effective mixing and storage containers, even for the perchloric acid."

"That's what I was afraid you'd say. Before you ask, no, I don't have a security system, and no, I don't have a closed-circuit TV system. All I've been doing up until now is to empty out the cash register at the end of the day and lock the doors behind me when I leave. In fact, it was only a few months ago that I added deadbolts to the front and back doors."

"How did the thief get in?" asked Julie.

"Back door. Looks like a crowbar or tire iron. Just about ripped the whole door off its hinges."

"Anything else you can tell us?" I asked. "Anything left behind, anything odd happen, anybody see or hear anything?"

"Hear, no. There was one odd thing though."

"Yes?"

"One of my buddies was teasing me the next day about my business not doing well and me having to trade-in my truck for an old beater."

"Looks like you're doing pretty well to me," I commented, gesturing around at the shop.

"That's the thing. Business has been great ever since the oil boom started. Suddenly we have all these young guys working the drill rigs and making great money. Most of them spend it as fast as it comes in, and one of the things they spend the money on is a new truck or SUV, and the next thing they want to do is add all kinds of chrome-plated accessories. In fact, chrome-plating is most of my business there days."

"What's the joke then?" asked Julie.

"Ah. Right. Well, my buddy happened to be driving down the street the night it happened, and he said there was an old, crappy-looking truck parked outside. He didn't see anyone but, since the lights were on inside the shop, he figured that it was me working in the shop. He just couldn't figure the truck."

"Did he describe it?"

"Sort of. Said it was an older model pickup truck, painted flat black, and not well done. More like someone with a few spray cans than the kind of job a bodyshop would do. That's why he called it a beater... and why he was teasing me about it."

"Did he happen to mention whether there was anything in the back of the truck?"

"In the back? No, I don't think so. I doubt he'd have spotted anything, anyway because he said there was a white cap on the back.... Oh. I guess I should have told you that, huh?"

"That's OK," I assured him, "you're been very helpful."

A few more questions satisfied us that we'd learned about all we were going to at the shop, so we thanked the manager and left.

"He's either getting bolder or sloppier, or both," I commented as Julie and I walked to our trucks.

"At least we know he's still using the same truck. Maybe someone else will spot it for us."

The next day, we drove to Dawson Creek, a small city of just over ten-thousand people. We made it there in under two hours and again checked-in at the local RCMP detachment. Everyone there had heard about our alert regarding the threat to the region's gas (and possibly oil) wells and the suspected vehicle, so we spent more time answering their questions of us than the other way around. The good news was that everyone seemed to be alert and taking the threat seriously.

Rather than just sit around and wait, I decided we might as well go visit some of the well sites ourselves and get acquainted with the area. Most of the oil and gas exploration and production activities at that time lie either to the northwest, towards Fort St. John, or to the south, but that still meant there was a large area to cover. Nevertheless, we spent the afternoon driving around. As expected, we spotted many drilling rigs in action, some oil wells, and a huge number of gas wells.

By 5 pm, half an hour past dusk, it was getting dark. Cold and tired, we decided we'd had enough for one day and were driving back to town when it happened.

There was a tremendous blast, the sky seemed to light up, and then I could feel the police truck shake when the pressure wave hit us. Julie and I immediately pulled over to the side of the road and got out to take a look. There, probably less than a kilometre away was a cone of orange flame that rose and expanded, then culminated in a kind of roiling fireball with tendrils of black smoke.

I ran back to my truck to send a quick report in by radio. I was only able to give a general idea of the location, since I didn't know the area well, but I assured the dispatcher that the towering cone of flame would point the way clearly enough for the emergency response crews to find it. I also put in a request for roadblocks to be set-up on the main roads out of the area, and to be on the lookout for a black pickup truck with a white cap on the back.

After that, I grabbed a flashlight and map so we could figure out just where we were. With the map spread out on the hood, we figured out our location and looked at the surrounding roads.

"Remember the observation point the bomber set-up at the Stony Plain pumpstation?" I asked Julie.

"Sure. He was set-up at about 150 yards. Sorry, I still think in American units. Nearly 140 metres."

"Right. So it might be that he chose the cover and it happened to be 140 metres, but it might have been the best cover at his preferred distance. Suppose he's a hunter, and not a marksman. In that case, he's probably used to using his rifle and scope in the 90 to 180 metre range."

"So, you want to try driving the local roads that are about that distance?"

"Yes. The local police and fire responders will do everything that can be done at the wellsite. I think our job is to search for the bomber."

And that's what we did. There were only a few roads, and a couple of access tracks, that passed within 200 metres of the gas well. The well, for its part, was still burning fiercely and putting up a vertical column of flame that served as a brilliant beacon against the rapidly darkening sky and the beginnings of a snow storm. We carefully drove all the roads, but were forced to conclude that the bomber had left, assuming that this was the work of our bomber and not simply an industrial accident.

Things didn't work out well regarding the roadblocks either. It turned out that the detachment was short-staffed at the time and already had some officers out on other calls. Of course, several units were sent to the fire scene to lend assistance, keep the general public away, and provide local traffic control so emergency vehicles could come and go. By the time a couple of units were finally dispatched to set up a few roadblocks, it was too little, too late.

To make matters worse, from our point of view, the division COs for B.C. and Alberta were unwilling to set-up highway checkpoints without some reliable intelligence on which direction our bomber was most likely to be heading. Since we had no idea, we couldn't get approval for the large number of resources that would be required.

We were, however, able to get two concessions. Our description of the man and vehicle, such as they were, were circulated to all detachments in both provinces, and we also got approval to have Air Services fly the main routes out of town in hopes of spotting the truck.

Unfortunately, the latter was foiled by the appearance of a blizzard overnight. That didn't ground the aircraft, but it made it unsafe for the aircraft to be able to fly low enough to have a realistic chance at spotting the vehicle.

All of that added up to one simple fact: we were on our own until the storm cleared.

That night, since we were snowbound anyway, Julie and I did some planning over dinner.

"He may simply have gone-to-ground somewhere, to hide out for a while, or else he's heading somewhere specific," I began. "He was so careless on that last break-in that I think he believes that he has us completely fooled, so he most likely simply set off the explosion and got out fast before anyone could get organized."

"In that case," put in Julie, "he's probably either heading home, wherever that is, or he's heading somewhere to prepare for his next threat."

I agreed. "Tomorrow, I think we can either go look for his vantage point by the burning well, or else check the gas stations and coffee shops along the main routes out of town. What do you think?"

"I vote for the second option," she said, almost immediately. "He may not have hung around any longer than he needed to take shot at his target. After all, he'd be vulnerable to being spotted after a rifle crack. Besides, I don't think we'd be likely to find even as much of a trace as we did at the last site. On the other hand, we might get lucky along the highways and find someone that has seen him, which could give us a better description than we have right now."

"I agree, and we really need to know which way he's headed if we don't want to just sit back and wait for the next threatening letter.

"So, there are five main roads out. Highway 97 in two branches, one heading northwest and the other southwest, Highway 2 heading southeast towards Grande Prairie, or one of two secondary highways, one heading north and the other east."

In the end, we decided that Julie would cover the two Highway 97 branches while I would do the others. After supper, we drove to every gas station in Dawson Creek looking for a witness to the bombers truck, but with no success. We did, however, leave a note at each station asking the next day's morning staff to phone the local RCMP detachment if they spotted anything resembling the truck.

The last things we learned, before retiring that night, were that several people working at a nearby wellsite reported hearing a rifle shot just before the explosion, and that the bomb blast had ruptured the 'Christmas tree[43]' at the wellhead, and created a 2-metre-wide crater beneath it. A specialized well-blowout company had been called-in to extinguish the fire and cap the well but, in the meantime, the fire would continue to burn.

The Daily News

Tuesday, December 18, 1979

Gas Well Explosion
Near Dawson Creek, B.C.

7 HUNTING

December 18, 1979

It was impossible to know how far to drive each route, so we had to make guesses. I decided that we should do as much as we could in a single day. Longer than that and the odds of anyone remembering a single truck driving along the highway would be remote, indeed. Working back from a planned rendezvous in Grande Prairie at about dusk, that gave Julie about three hours to spend on each branch of Highway 97 before driving back, while I could afford to spend about the same amount of time on each of the secondary roads. That meant we'd each be driving Highway 2 east to Grande Prairie as our last leg, but only I would make the stops on that segment.

As it turned out, we didn't have to do the entire plan. I'd covered the secondary roads as far as time allowed, and was making my way along Highway 2 when I got a lead. I had stopped at a big highway service station, in the middle of nowhere, where a gas-bar attendant that had worked the previous day's evening shift actually remembered a truck matching our description.

"Kind of a weaselly-looking guy," the attendant related. "He didn't say much, I don't think. Just got a fill and paid in cash. The reason I remember him is the truck. Flat black, and it had the worst paint-job I've ever seen, and I've seen some bad ones. He must have just bought some of those little aerosol paint cans and gone to it. No surface preparation, no dust booth, just sprayed everything leaving obvious seams and overlaps, and everything. It was so bad, he might just as well have used a paint brush!"

"Did you happen to notice the licence plates?"

"Ontario plates," he replied without hesitation. "I only noticed because I was looking at the bad paint job, but they were Ontario plates. No question."

The attendant had more good news as well. He thought that the man had gone into the station's café to eat. "They might remember him there," he concluded.

They did.

The café had a single cook and a single server, but the latter had been working long shifts to save up for college and had actually been on duty the previous evening. It hadn't been busy because of the storm, and she remembered that one of their few customers matched our description. From her description of the customer's coat and hat, among other things, it was almost certainly the same person that the gas-bar attendant remembered. She remembered his personality too.

"Cranky," she said. "Cranky and cheap. He didn't talk much though. When I asked where he was going, he just said 'East.' He paid his bill in cash – bills and coins – and he counted out the exact change to the penny. No tip. When I asked him if something had been wrong with his meal, he claimed I hadn't been nice enough. I ask you? Not nice enough? 'Well, excuse me!' I said to him, but all he did was stalk out, muttering under his breath. Good riddance, I say."

The only things she'd been able to add to our growing description of the man was that he had brown eyes and medium-brown, but thinning, hair.

Thanking the server and the attendant, I returned to the police truck and radioed Julie to abort her search and come after me.

As Silver and I continued east on the highway, I didn't expect our bomber to need to stop again for some hours but I checked each service station and restaurant/coffee-shop along the way anyway. I was glad I did.

It was another of those big, highway-side service stations that seem to appear from out of nowhere, and that sit all by themselves along an otherwise long and deserted stretch of highway, far from the nearest towns on either side. As usual, it was a truck stop and had an attached coffee shop, probably a good one judging from the number of semi-trailer rigs parked outside.

Once again, it was a gas-bar attendant that remembered the truck, and it had been that very morning too.

"Yup. I remember that crappy-looking truck, the Ontario plates, and I remember the crotchety driver too. Pulled in here and said he only wanted to buy five litres of gas! Wanted it put in a plastic gas can, he said, because it was for a woman that had run out of gas a few kilometres back down the road. Our loaner gas can holds 20 litres, but no, he insisted I only put five litres into it. He paid in cash for the gas, but he refused to leave a deposit. We argued about that, because it's the company policy to require a deposit. In the end, he said I could hold his credit card until he got back. That seemed OK, so I let him get away with it."

The man looked suddenly embarrassed. "He scammed me though! When I looked at the name on the card after he left, it said he was a doctor. He didn't look like a doctor to me, so I tried putting the deposit on his card and guess what?"

"Let me guess. It had been cancelled."

"Damn right.... Excuse me, darn right. The message came back saying it was a stolen card. Made me feel like a fool."

I commiserated with him, especially since he'd been trying to help people out. "Is there anything else you can tell me?" I asked, not hoping for much. But I was wrong, there was more.

He never saw the man again, of course, but the woman, when she arrived, had been irate. She'd run out of gas a few kilometres before the station and had flagged down the next vehicle to come along, which was the black pickup truck with the white cap on the back. The man was practically forced to stop, because the woman stood right out in the centre of the lane waving her arms. A dangerous thing to do but, apparently, it worked. The man stopped, and after hearing her tale agreed to stop at the next station, get some gas, and bring it back to her.

The attendant related that the woman had been embarrassed and upset about being foolish enough to run out of gas on the highway, and in winter too, but what really upset her was that her 'Good Samaritan' hadn't been that good after all – he wanted to make a profit off of her!

"A profit?" I asked.

"The woman said that he'd only agreed to go the station if she gave him $50. She said that was about all she had on her, but she felt she was in no position to argue, so she gave it to him. When he came back and handed the gas can to her, she said it felt awfully light, but he said there was enough there to get her to the station. Well, he was right about that, but when she got here, I told her that he'd only bought 5 litres. 'Five litres!' she exclaimed. 'One gallon!' Yup. He'd charged her $50 for one-dollar's worth of gas[44]. She sure used a lot of colourful language at that point."

"Well, at least he did come and get some gas for her. Do you happen to know who she is, or where she lives?"

"No. Not a local anyway because I don't think I've ever seen her before... or her car either," he added after a moment's thought."

"Too bad. I'd like to learn more about this 'Samaritan.'"

"Is he the one you're looking for?"

"Could be, but we don't know for sure. That's why I'm trying to learn as much as I can."

"I really wish she was still here to talk to you then. At one point, she was even imitating his speech!"

"Oh?" I said. That sounded interesting. "What did he sound like?"

"I can't do the voice, and anyway, it wasn't like he had a foreign accent or anything. It was his manner that she was imitating. She said that, after she'd explained her problem and asked for his help, he'd said 'Sure, but it'll cost you,' in kind of an evil, sneaky voice. She repeated that more than once, as if trying to understand how someone could be so selfish."

"It's certainly not the Canadian way," I replied, but my mind had gone elsewhere. Something about that expression sounded familiar, but I didn't know why. We were learning something about our bomber's character and manner anyway, and I mentally added mean and larcenous to the list. Of course, these things paled in comparison with the bombings, the destruction, and the loss of life, but a profile was starting to come together.

While I was at the service station, I took the opportunity to phone Ottawa to update my boss, Bob, on the latest developments and to request help getting updated bulletins out to all of the detachments and municipal police departments in Alberta and

Saskatchewan.

Silver and I were still driving east, stopping at gas stations and coffee shops along the way, when Julie and Scout caught up to us. From that point on, we went together to Grande Prairie, where we spent the night.

The next day, we continued driving east and repeated our leap-frogging pattern of the day before. For most of the day Julie and I each found the same thing: nothing. No sightings, no colourful stories, no new leads. Our lack of success made is seem longer and more tiring than it should have, but we persevered.

Once again, it was just when a sense of futility was settling-in on us that we got lucky at a service station on the outskirts of Edmonton. One of the attendants remembered "the crappy-looking truck" and "the cranky man." Apparently, he was still memorable. The attendant didn't observe anything we didn't already know, but said that the man had asked about the road conditions towards the east. When he'd asked where the man was going, he'd said Saskatchewan, but hadn't offered anything more specific.

That was a good break for us, and I immediately called Bob in Ottawa again to specifically ask highway patrol units along the highway to the east to be extra vigilant.

As we were thanking the attendant and preparing to leave, she said "Would you like to see the truck for yourselves?"

"See it?"

It turned out that the station had recently installed video-surveillance cameras at their self-serve gas bars to combat the increasing problem of people driving away without paying for their gas. The cameras were only black and white, of course, and the recording was done on VHS videotapes.

"Each camera feeds its own recorder," the attendant explained, "and a single EP-type tape will hold six hours-worth, so we start them at the beginning of the morning shift, change tapes after six hours, then again after another six, and then once more, which takes us up to closing time. Then, we record over the old tapes the next day. Your fellow came through here this morning, so he should show up on one of the morning tapes."

She led us into the office, where there were banks of monitors with tapes being recorded. There was also a standalone videocassette recorder and monitor duo that enabled us to view the morning tapes. After fast-forwarding through two tapes without success, the attendant found our suspect's truck on the third tape.

"There it is," she said, triumphantly, as she pressed the pause switch.

Sure enough, it looked like our truck all right. The camera view was from above and behind the truck, and showed the truck, the pump, and a clock that was strategically positioned on a nearby pillar. As intended, the image provided a clear view of the rear of the vehicle, the licence plate, and the time. The tailgate had a Chevrolet logo on it, so that was something too. After we'd written-down the licence plate number (and verified that it was an Ontario plate), play was resumed and we could see a figure emerge from the truck. Unfortunately, it only showed someone wearing a jacket with its hood up and walking with a slight stoop – just like we'd seen the last time he'd been caught on a security camera. After the tank had been filled, the man walked back to the driver's door from the rear of the vehicle, so we never did get a view from his front.

Thanking the attendant, I asked if we could borrow the tape for a while, for which I wrote her out a receipt. Meanwhile, Julie telephoned CPIC with the licence plate number and the make of the truck, telling them that we'd call back in a few hours to learn whether they had been able to find a match.

Two hours later, when Julie called-in to CPIC, she discovered that the licence plate number got a hit. It was reportedly stolen from a car in Sudbury, Ontario, on or about November 11. That certainly fit with our thinking, as the TransCanada Highway from Ottawa to Winnipeg went through Sudbury.

CPIC also reported a large number of Chevrolet pickup trucks stolen in Ontario around that time, so that wasn't much help for us, especially since we didn't know whether the truck had been stolen at all. An older truck could simply have been purchased in a personal, cash transaction somewhere, and then not registered by the new owner.

It had been a long day, so we stayed overnight in Edmonton. In the middle of the night, my bedside clock said it was just past 2 am when I woke up from a deep sleep and realized that I'd been dreaming about something to do with the bomber. Apparently, my subconscious mind had continued to try to piece together the various clues we'd been picking up. I wasn't surprised, as I'd come to realize that this kind of thing was an occupational hazard for me. The good news was that, in exchange for the loss of sleep, my subconscious was sometimes able to detect patterns that eluded my conscious mind.

In this case, unfortunately, I couldn't remember any specifics from my dream. I was positive that it had something to do with our suspect and the episode of the lady that ran out of gas. I knew that my subconscious was probably replaying what I'd learned, trying to make sense out of it, and that what it added to the story was probably just imagination, but something in the dream had struck a chord. Maybe enough of a chord to pull me out of my sleep. But what?

I tried to bring back whatever I'd been dreaming about, but there was nothing. Then, something went 'click' and a horrible suspicion crept into my mind. As it did, I could see how the whole series of bomb-related events might make a crazy kind of sense.

The next morning, I telephoned CPIC myself with a very different kind of information request. I had an answer within minutes. If I was right, it left me with just one outstanding quandary, but it was a huge one. When I brought Julie up-to-date at breakfast the next morning, I ended by saying: "The big questions now are where will he strike next and is there any way we can get ahead of him? Otherwise, we'll just keep on showing up at places he's already chosen and prepared in advance."

"OK," she said. "But how?"

"I think we'll have to guess."

"Guess?"

"Make an educated guess then, based on his patterns so far and the available targets."

"It still seems like trying to find a needle in a haystack."

"It is, but until Ottawa receives another threatening letter, I think we can afford some time following intuition, or hunches, if you like. But first we need to know more about where he's heading next. Let's start by assuming that he stayed in this city overnight, that he stayed somewhere that's very affordable, and that's still used to a lot of cash-paying customers."

Edmonton had a few hotels, and a large number of motels that fit that description, so Julie and I spent several hours phoning around and asking whether any of them recognized the descriptions of our suspect or his truck. One did. The man in question had stayed only the one night, paid in cash, and left several hours earlier.

"He gave his name as Frank Smith and an Ontario address," said Julie, when she got off the phone from her conversation with the motel at which he'd been seen.

"Did they notice anything else?" I asked.

"Just one thing, he was cranky"

"Sounds like our suspect all right. I don't suppose he told them where he was going?"

That produced Julie's brilliant smile. "Not exactly," she said, "but they remembered him asking for directions to Highway 16."

"The Yellowhead Highway, that means he's continuing east towards Lloydminster."

"Right," continued Julie.

"Hmmm. OK, so imagine you're the bomber. You're not trying to kill masses of people, not target any particular industry, and it's not for extortion – it's more like you're sending signals and enjoying your power. You've been making small bombs, all things considered, and you like using them to hit, or at least threaten, things that explode into large fireballs. So far, you've hit a train carrying explosive fuels, an oil pipeline, and a natural gas well. What else might attract you?"

She thought for a moment. "Refineries, chemical plants, explosives manufacturers?"

"Yes. It's interesting that there is a big refinery and a big chemical plant right here, in the northeast corner of Edmonton, yet he seems to have left this morning, heading for Saskatchewan. Why?"

"I don't know, but he seems to like moving around. Maybe it's to make sure he stays well ahead of us? For his own safety, I mean. Or, maybe he likes making us follow him all around the country."

"It could be a combination of both. But now we seem to be backtracking. First, it was Ontario, then southern Alberta, then central Alberta, then northern BC, and now we seem to be passing through Alberta and heading for Saskatchewan. I can't help wondering whether his next target is going to be in Saskatchewan or Manitoba. My instincts say Saskatchewan."

"OK. Why Saskatchewan? Because he hasn't struck there yet?"

"Indirectly…. Julie, you're going to think I'm crazy, but I need to tell you a story."

I told her about my dream. Then I told her where it had led my thoughts.

Julie called CPIC, to get the name and address searched, while I made some calls regarding the address that had been given. We knew that the man may have given false information, but it had to be checked.

Julie reported that there were no hits from CPIC on the name or address, while I discovered that the address corresponded to a restaurant in Sudbury. The address was real but, according to the utility companies, no one lived there. That's the way it goes, sometimes.

An hour later, we were on the highway heading east. I had a feeling that a showdown was coming.

Laurie Schramm

8 CONVERGENCE

Despite the surly impression he made on others, Frank Smith was well satisfied He'd hit the package properly with his first shot and the gas well had exploded beautifully. Although he'd left the scene immediately, he'd stuck to back roads and secondary highways to the extent possible, and if the police had set-up road-blocks, they'd either done it too late or in the wrong places. He was heading now for Lloydminster, where he would replenish his ammonium nitrate supply, and make his last two explosive devices.

He had two more strikes planned. He might or might not explode the first bomb- he'd decide that later- but the second one would be his last, after which his quest would be complete. Only then would he recover the last of the cache of gold coins at his cabin and go find place to retire.

Maybe I'll go to Alaska, he thought to himself. The kind of place where people could be alone without raising eyebrows, and where he wouldn't be recognized.

***

It was nominally a two-and-a-half-hour drive from Edmonton to Lloydminster and the Saskatchewan border, but it took us longer because we continued to stop at gas stations and coffee shops along the way to check for sightings of Frank Smith or his truck. We did it efficiently, at least, with Julie and I alternating in the task of checking at each place, and then leap-frogging over the other so that each of us only checked each second location.

It was only when we got to Vermillion, about three-quarters of the way there, that our diligence was rewarded. A service station attendant remembered "a crotchety old guy in a crappy old truck." As the attendant couldn't have been more than sixteen years old, I imagined that he thought I was pretty old too. He took an active interest in Silver however, which seemed to dispose him to talk to me readily enough.

In any case, upon questioning, he hadn't noticed the licence plates but his description of the man and the truck matched what we had so far on Frank Smith and his black and white truck. The last bit of information I got was that the man had asked the attendant how much further it was to "Lloyd," meaning Lloydminster. That meant we were still on Frank Smith's trail.

Although Julie and I continued our leap-frogging each other and checking out the last few service stations and cafes, we didn't get any additional leads and soon rolled into Lloydminster, where we checked into a motel and then the local RCMP Detachment.

With a population of just over ten-thousand people[45], the detachment had a nominal staffing of 15 Members, with a Staff-Sergeant as the Officer in Charge (OiC). As luck would have it, we were able to get in to see the OiC right away, and briefed him on our case and the latest developments, winding-up with a request that the city and highway patrols be asked to keep a lookout for the black and white truck.

After that, with most of the day gone, we took the dogs for a walk, then dinner, then turned-in for an early night.

After breakfast the next morning, we were back in our rooms when I received a telephone call from the detachment. It was the OiC himself.

"Thought you might like to know," he began, "I was reading last night's shift reports and there was a break-in that might interest you."

"Yes?"

"Around 2 am someone broke into one of the local farm-supply stores, but it's odd, because whoever it was didn't seem to have made any attempt to break into the cash registers. All they did was grab a bag of fertilizer and run. It sounds like your kind of thing, so I thought you might want to check it out."

I assured him that I certainly did, noted down the store's name and address, and thanked him. I won't go through the whole episode here, basically, Julie and I visited the store, inspected the point of break-in, clarified what was stolen and asked about anything that might help identify the thief.

It turned out that the store had a silent alarm with an auto-dialer that phoned the store manager and played a recorded tape saying that the intrusion alarm had been triggered. The manager had called the police and then gone himself to investigate, which he really shouldn't have done of course. He should have let the police deal with it. Since the manager lived very close to the store, he was the first on the scene and saw a black pickup truck with a white cap driving away. Whether the thief realized an alarm had been tripped or not, they broke-in quickly, grabbed a bag of fertilizer quickly, and then left quickly. That was all the information we were able to gain, but it seemed to indicate that Frank Smith was in town and replenishing his supply of bomb-making supplies.

"What do you want to do?" Julie asked

"I think he's going to strike the refinery next. He's here, and he's accumulating materials for more bombs. It's exactly the kind of thing he likes to hit: big, huge explosion and fire potential, possibly not too much risk of killing people if he does it right, and something he can detonate from a reasonable distance so he can get away. So, we need to plan, and we'll need to get some help."

Our next step was to go see the refinery manager.

Lloydminster's refinery is specialized in that it uses asphalt as a feedstock, the asphalt being locally mined. Its products range from various grades of paving asphalt, to kerosene, to other distillates and fuels, including diesel. At 27,000 barrels per day (4,300 m^3/d), it's a small refinery, as most Canadian refineries process three to six times as many barrels per day. It was positioned just outside the southeast corner of the city, which made sense since the prevailing winds would be from the west.

The refinery looked huge to us, as we drove up to the sprawling complex. Even a drive around the perimeter took us a long time, but it was enough to tell us that the complex was approximately square in shape, just over a kilometre on each side, therefore covering an area of about two-and-a-half square kilometres.

When we explained our concerns to the refinery manager, he politely heard us out, but it was obvious that he wasn't very concerned, given the absence of a specific threat. He did agree to have someone drive us around the complex, and he said he would speak to his security people about increasing their vigilance, but we were left feeling that little would be done to actually increase security.

The young engineer that was assigned to show us around was helpful enough, however, especially once he got over the shock of learning why we were there. He, at least, didn't spend any time questioning the probability and leapt straight to the possible threat.

"You can pretty much take your pick," he said "There are a huge number of vulnerable places within the refinery complex itself: everything from pipelines, to distillation towers, to the storage tanks. I doubt the incoming asphalt would be struck though. Why try to make asphalt burn when you can go after diesel or kerosene and really put on a show?"

He drove us around in a large van that easily held all of us, including the dogs, and even gave Julie and I each a map of the refinery complex so we could better visualize the placement of things as we went around. The complex was essentially comprised of seven more-or-less adjacent zones arranged from south to north. Starting from the south end of the complex, there was:

- o a massive parking lot, in which ten rows could hold about a thousand employee and contractor vehicles,
- o a double row of long office and/ or storage 'portables', truck-transportable building units, with about thirty portables in each row,
- o a large lay-down area, in which major components like pipes, pumps, vessels and so forth could be stored and/ or assembled,
- o a cluster of utility buildings to provide power, water, and steam distribution,
- o the refining area proper. This seemed to be a veritable jungle of storage tanks, mixing and hydrocracking units, and distillation towers. Everything was interconnected by a myriad of large pipelines, most of which ran overhead so it was possible to drive under them,
- o large settling basins, not all in one place, but arranged around three sides of the refining area. I counted at least

seven as we drove around, and

o nearly twenty medium- and large-sized oil storage tanks. At
   least six of the storage tanks appeared to be of the 30
   metre (100 ft.) diameter by 9 metre (30 ft.) tall type,
   meaning they could each hold as much as 6,672 cubic
   metres (42,000 barrels).

Looking at all the oil-storage tanks I couldn't help thinking,
with a shudder, that each of those tanks could hold more oil, diesel,
or kerosene than any one of the oil cars on the train that Frank
Smith had derailed less than six weeks earlier, with catastrophic
results.

There were publicly-accessible roads running along the north
and west sides, a rail line along the east side, and a major highway
not far from the northeast corner. On the south side, a public road
led to the huge parking lot, but everything else lay within a high
security fence, and were accessible only by being checked through a
well-guarded security gate.

Our tour guide explained that employees and contractors alike
had to park in the main parking lot and then board shuttle buses to
be taken onto the refinery site proper. Each shuttle had to stop at
the security gate and have each person's identification checked and
logged. Once inside, the shuttles could take people wherever they
need to go. Service, delivery, and contractor vehicles that were
required to access the site had to show a special pass to get through
the security gate.

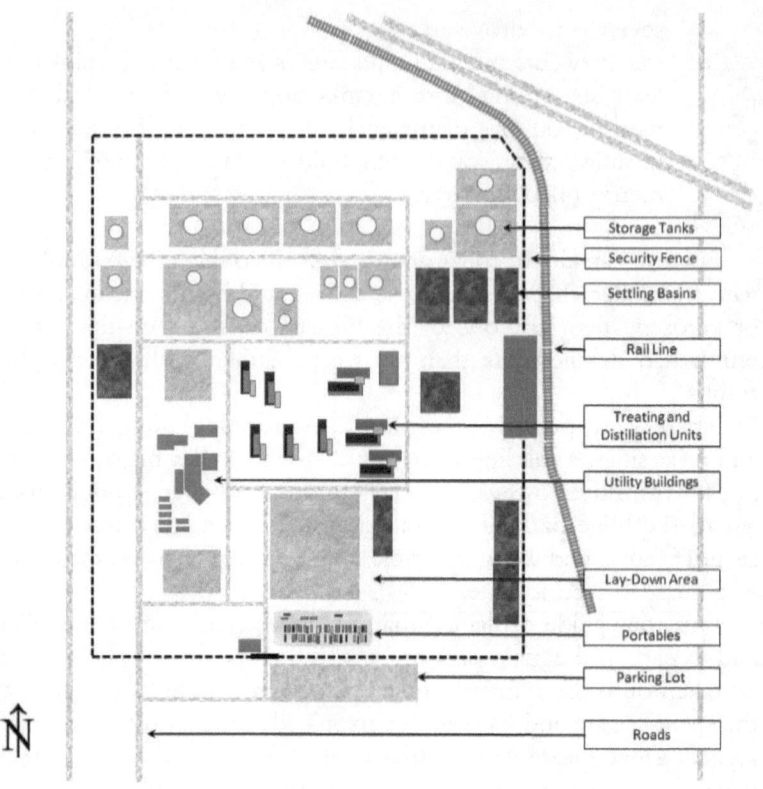

When Julie and I went off to discuss what we had learned, we had already each come to the same conclusion.

"One of the oil tanks," said Julie, sounding sure of herself.

"Why?" I asked, playing Devil's advocate.

"It would take some time to figure out how to bluff his way past the security gate and even if he did, it would be hard to be inconspicuous. If he were to place a bomb under one of the service or contractor vehicles it would be unlikely to end up in a location he could spot and target with his rifle. Also, that would potentially kill more people, which he apparently doesn't want to do. That eliminates the refining units and the interior pipeline corridors. The utility and other buildings don't meet his pattern and are too hard to get at anyway. That leaves oil cars on the rail sidings, exterior pipelines, and the oil tanks themselves, for which he'd have to scale or break through the fence and sneak onto the grounds on foot."

"OK, I agree. Why the oil tanks in particular then?"

"Pattern again. He's already taken out rail cars and shown he can take out pipelines. To the extent that at least some of all this has to do with ego and power, then oil tanks are something new. Plus, they look like the easiest to get at, probably have the least vigilant security measures. In addition, there are empty fields on those two sides of the complex so he'd have lots of scope to find a suitable hiding place from which to target the bomb.... Oh, and one more thing: if he sets off one of those really big tanks, and its nearly full, and the contents are something like diesel or kerosene, then he'll create the biggest fireball yet"

"I think you have it, Julie. We can't totally ignore the other target possibilities but I agree the oil tanks seem like the most obvious next target. Too bad there are so many of them."

"Do you still think the refinery is the next target?"

"Same answer. It seems like the most likely, based on what little we really know. Besides, we might just as well assume it's the refinery than pick something else at random, and until we get new information, I'd rather we did something than do nothing."

"Just us again, I suppose," said Julie with a slight sigh.

"Seems like it We can't really expect the local detachment to supply extra resources without a more clearly defined threat, and all we have are possible sightings of possibly the right person, our own analysis of Smith's patterns, and intuition. Meanwhile, the refinery manager doesn't really believe anyone would actually attack his refinery, and I don't see how we're going to change his mind without a clear and specific threat."

"The way you put it, it does sound far-fetched."

"Yes, but you and I think he's here, so here we'll stay. For now, anyway."

That same afternoon, I received a radio message to phone my boss, Bob, in Ottawa. Bob had news: they'd just received another letter in that day's mail. It had been constructed in the same manner as the previous ones, and was similarly brief: "HOW ABOUT A REFINERY." Presumably he hadn't been able to find a question mark to cut out and paste into the letter.

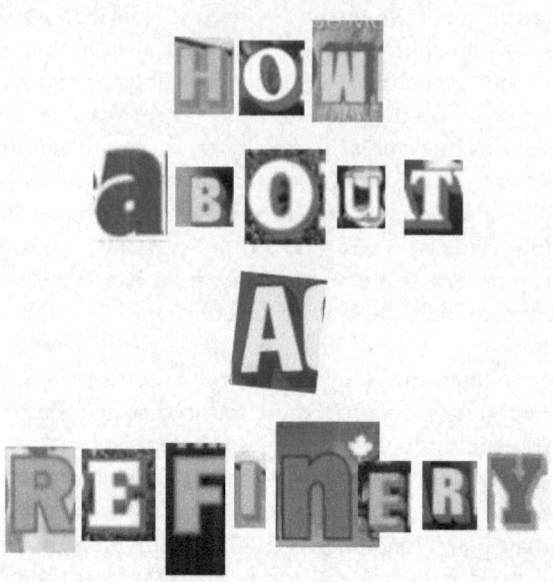

I told Bob why we had already come to the same conclusion, and which refinery we thought it was going to be.

"You're not going to get much local help without something more specific," Bob mused.

"I know," I agreed. "Can you get us some air support at least?"

"Probably, but it might take some time to get an aircraft out to where you are. Call me back in an hour and I should have some answers for you."

An hour later, I received Bob's news: it would take some time to get an aircraft to Lloydminster, so there would be no surveillance help that day. On the other hand, I could have as many flights a day as I wanted for the next three days subject only to pilot-hour restrictions and assuming sufficient visibility. That wasn't as much as I'd asked for, but more than I'd realistically hoped for, and I was genuine in my thanks.

After relaying the latest news to Julie, I said: "We'll have to talk to the pilot and spotter tonight or tomorrow morning, but I'm thinking we should ask for as many dawn-to-dusk flights as they're willing and able to fly, at the highest altitude that would still allow them to spot Frank Smith's truck, and that they only fly in more-or less-straight lines; no obvious circling."

"Sounds good," she replied "The fields bordering the tank farm are pretty barren, so a man could hide but the truck should be easy to spot."

"Yes. As long as we're right and he doesn't go to the east side and try for a rail car."

"Do you think the refinery manager will listen to us now that we have the threat letter?"

"No. I don't really. It doesn't specify which refinery. We have to try, but I think he's just going to tell us how many oil refineries there are in Canada and bid us good day."

We did go to meet once more with the refinery manager. As expected, he heard us out, thanked us for the update and for our concern, and then showed us the door. His only concession was to write-out special vehicle passes for each of us, granting us unlimited access to the refinery for the next three days.

"Well, that was about as helpful as we thought it would be," I commented as Julie and I walked to our SUVs.

"We did learn something new though," said Julie, trying to be positive. "We now know that there are 39 oil refineries[46] in Canada!"

That forced me to laugh, and I reflected on how great it was to be working with her again.

"I guess we're on our own then," she added

"On our own. Yes. You know, the best thing about being a dog handler in the Force is the independence of working alone so often. Far from the office, with its administration and office politics. The worst thing is that sometimes it's better to work as part of a team, not just you and your dog, but a larger team."

"Well, that's what you have Scout and I for. Isn't it?" said Julie brightly.

That got me chuckling again. "OK You win. Let's see if we can catch our Mister Smith this time. Just the four of us."

"So, what's next boss?"

"Well, the threat letter was sent and received, and we're both sure that the target refinery is right here. Mister Smith probably has his next bomb ready by now, and I think we have to assume that he'll try to place it tonight or tomorrow night. If he hasn't done it already, that is.

"Let's let the dogs sweep each of the big oil tanks, then the rail cars, and then spot check as many other areas as we have time for. After dinner, we'll have to go to the airport and meet the pilots when the police plane lands. After that, I think we might as well divide up and just drive the roads around the refinery's perimeter until dusk."

We had Silver and Scout check as many areas as we could. I even gave them a reminder sniff of the blanket we'd found at the Stony Plain pump station and had them sweep the parking lot. It all led to the same thing: nothing.

When we met the pilots, we discussed plans for the next three days and they agreed to do what I'd asked, with the two of them taking turns flying and spotting.

In the evening, Julie and I tried driving the roads around the refinery perimeter but didn't spot anything suspicious. When it became dark, we even went back to our motel and called all of the local hotels and motels without turning up anything on a Frank Smith or an older black and white truck, although we were fully aware that both the name and truck could have been changed by then.

It was all very discouraging.

The next morning, we'd just finished breakfast and were about to drive to the refinery when I received a phone call from the refinery manager. Their security people had found a break in their fence on the northwest side of the complex, by the tank farm.

"If it's our man, then he's planted a bomb in there somewhere. Clear the area and we'll have the dogs do a sweep."

The manager agreed and said he'd meet us on the public road outside the fence.

After alerting Julie, I called the Staff-Sergeant OiC at the local RCMP detachment to bring him up to date.

"Sounds like you were right all along," he said. "Do you need anything right now?"

"Not for the moment," I replied. "But if we find something, I'll call it in along with a request for backup, so we can establish an evacuation perimeter, and for the nearest bomb squad."

"The nearest bomb squad is in Edmonton. I'll give them a call now so they're alerted but they won't come all this way unless you find something specific."

"I know. If we find something, we'll wait it out"

As I thanked him and hung up the phone, Julie appeared in my doorway. "Ready?" she asked.

"Ready. The refinery manager will meet us on the public road near the northwest comer of the property. When we get there, let's bring the hand-held radios this time." We hadn't been using the Motorola hand-held VHF radios we'd borrowed much because they added unwelcome bulk and weight to all the other gear we carried. This time, however, I had a feeling we were going to need them.

Laurie Schramm

9 WALK INTO MY PARLOUR[47]

A light snow was beginning to fall as we parked our SUVs at the side of the public road by the refinery. Beside us was a shallow ditch, a strip of grass, then the refinery's security fence. The refinery manager and one of his security people were waiting to meet us at the roadside. When introductions were complete, the manager pointed to a spot where, even from the road, we could see that the fence had been cut both vertically and horizontally and then peeled back to create a person-sized gap in the shape of an inverted V.

"Is that how you found it?' I asked.

"Exactly like that," the security man answered. "We haven't disturbed anything."

"It's not very subtle," I commented. "I would have expected him to fold the sides back again after he left to disguise the breach."

"Is that important?" asked the manager.

"Maybe not. It just looks odd to me, that's all."

"Shall we?' said the manager, pointing to the fence again and gesturing with one arm.

"Yes, but if you don't mind, let's let the dogs go first."

After Julie and I had gathered our gear, including radios for both of us and a daypack for me, we instructed Silver and Scout to search for explosives and sent them ahead on long leads.

Nothing remarkable happened as we crossed the ditch and grass, then approached the fence. When we arrived at the gap in the fence Silver, however, spent more time than Scout sniffing and growling around the ground right in front of the breach.

"What's he growling about?" asked the security man. "There isn't a bomb here is there?" I could hear the apprehension in his voice. Our bomb-threat concerns had become very real to the refinery people all of a sudden.

"No, it's nothing related to explosives. He's trained to give a different signal for that. It's something else." I went up to Silver and knelt down to peer into his eyes. "What is it, Silver?"

I sensed... anger. There was something about the scents here that he recognized and didn't like.

"OK Silver," I said, and patted him on the shoulder. "I hear you, but let's keep searching," and Julie and I signalled the dogs to keep looking for explosives.

As we squeezed through the fence and continued to follow the dogs, I could hear the sound of an airplane high overhead.

"Twin-engine, propeller-driven," said Julie, who had her binoculars out and had spotted the plane.

"Police plane," I explained to the others. "They're looking for our suspect's truck. They'll make periodic passes as long as the visibility allows."

In front of us were two of the smaller oil storage tanks. Not far behind them, I knew, were the really big ones. The dogs sniffed around here and there, looking for telltale scents, but again, while Scout seemed to find nothing of interest, Silver had caught some kind of scent, that led him- and us- all the way around first one tank and then the other.

"Are you sure these dogs are any good?" asked the manager. "One of them doesn't seem to smell anything and the other is just growling and going in circles."

"Trust us," I said. "Silver and I have been working together for four years, and he's very, very good. If he's found something of concern, then I'm concerned. But whatever it is, it's not explosives, it's something else. Anyway, let's keep going."

As we set the dogs in motion again, Julie came alongside of me and raised a questioning eyebrow.

"Games," I growled, realizing as I did that I was beginning to sound like Silver. "I don't like this. We're being led by the nose."

Sure enough, while Scout's search pattern comprised broad sweeps from side to side, Silver seemed to be following a scent trail, and he was heading towards one of the really big oil storage tanks. As soon as I recognized this, I called a halt, and asked the manager and security man to stay where they were while Julie and I continued forward.

"You really think there's a bomb there?" the manager asked, torn between curiosity and fear now.

"Let's just keep our risks down, OK?"

Julie and I continued onwards. It wasn't long before Silver and Scout had reached the edge of the berm that formed the wall of the tank's secondary containment pit. This was kind of like a broad moat surrounding the tank, and designed to contain the oil should there be a leak.

We signalled for the dogs to keep going and they went over the berm, then down and across the pit to the tank itself. After a bit of sniffing here and there, both dogs ended up standing at the bottom of the spiral staircase that led to the top of the tank, and looking up at the stairway.

"Let's have a look from here," I said, digging out my own binoculars. As Julie and I used our binoculars to scan the stairway, we moved some distance to one side and then the other until Julie said: "There. Underneath one step, about a third of the way up the stairs we can see, by that patch of metal that looks almost like a door."

"I see it," I said, as I found what she had spotted: a small circle that was bright orange in colour. "Looks like the trademark bright orange cap to me," I said.

"Should we get a closer look?" she asked.

"He's probably watching us right now, so let's not tempt fate. I think we should set some other wheels in motion."

We called the dogs back to us and returned to the spot where we'd left the refinery manager and the security man.

"Find anything?" he asked, as we approached.

"Is there any reason why you'd have a bright orange object, round and about three to four inches in diameter, tucked under one of the spiral staircase stairs on that tank?"

"None" he said.

"Well, the explosive devices we've been finding consist of two bottles taped together, one of which always has a bright orange cap on it. Our bomber uses it as a sighting target, and when he puts a bullet through it, that creates the detonation. I think that's what's attached to your tank's stairway. We'd go up for a closer look, but I suspect he's out there watching us through a rifle-scope."

This was coming pretty fast, but he seemed to be keeping up. "OK," he said, "what do you want us to do?" ·

"Let's just step over here, if you don't mind." I led everyone to a spot where I estimated that we'd be blocked from external view by one of the smaller oil tanks. "OK, if he's here, he's out in one of those two fields to the northwest, probably with a hunting rife and a scope, and probably pretty well hidden. Right here, we should be out of his sight for the moment. So. Please keep the area clear and call the fire department. I imagine you have some of your staff cross-trained so they can respond to emergencies on site?"

"Yes. We have some on every shift."

"Great. I'd call them in now. We'll radio the local RCMP Detachment. Then, I'll have one more request. By the way, what's in that particular tank?"

"Diesel. The tank's about half full."

Great, I thought to myself.

As we stepped away a few steps to give each other some space, the manager used his company radio to send an alarm code to their emergency responders, while the security man used his to call for reinforcements from his own unit. While they were doing that, I asked Julie to contact the Staff Sergeant at the local detachment, on the standard RCMP channel, while I radioed the police plane on another, prearranged channel.

"Charlie, Frank, Mike, Papa, November, from Echo 007," I called, using the aviation industry's standard phonetic alphabet to spell out the police plane's registration code: C-FMPN[48].

"Charlie, Frank, Mike, go ahead Echo Seven," came an acknowledgement, abbreviating our codes.

"What's your twenty?"

"We just took off and were about to head for your target site for a pass."

"Perfect. We have located a possible explosive device on one of the tanks in the northwest comer. Can you look specifically at the area to the northwest of the compound that would have a direct line of sight to the three oil tanks that lie in the extreme northwest corner?"

"10-4, Echo Seven," they responded, "we are 10-17."

"Advise caution Charlie, Frank, Mike. We assess realistic possibility that an explosive device on the larger tank may be remotely detonated by suspect, by gunshot."

"10-4, Echo Seven. We will keep to the northwest."

When we had all finished with our radio calls, Julie, the refinery manager, and the security guy reconvened. The latter two said they would deal with matters on site and receive the incoming fire and police vehicles. I told them that Julie and the dogs and I were going to try hunting down the suspect, assuming that he was still in the area.

"You mentioned having one more request," the manager said, before leaving.

Before I could answer I heard the sound of a rifle shot, and was just in the middle of yelling "Get down!" when there was a tremendous explosion, the shock wave from which knocked us all to the ground anyway, which was fortunate because several large pieces of metal flew over our heads and landed nearby.

As I twisted around to look back, I could see some kind of dark liquid pouring out of the tank. It was burning brightly, having been ignited by the explosion.

As we all pulled ourselves together and got up, we moved further away from the fire.

"What was the request?" the manager repeated, staring in disbelief at the raging fire.

"Can you loan us a vehicle? It will probably only be for a few hours."

"Something wrong with yours?"

"No, but I'd like to leave ours where they are for now. I have an idea I'd like to test."

"Sure. Take my truck. It's right there." He pointed to a company truck with amber flashing lights.

Leaving them to deal with things on the refinery site, Julie and I loaded the dogs into the manager's truck which, fortunately, had a roomy crew-cab. Then Julie radioed the detachment to update them on the explosion, ask them to cancel the bomb squad, and send help. Meanwhile, I put in a radio call to the Twin Otter.

"We see it Echo Seven. The smoke is blowing to the east, so we'll continue our sweep."

"Why the truck?" asked Julie, when she was done with her call.

"Because I'm worried," I admitted. "Don't you think this was all just a bit too easy?"

"Easy?"

"Not the past month, this particular situation. Look, he probably figures we were able to follow him to Lloydminster, but I hope he doesn't know how much we've really learned. Then, he does a break-in right here, the same town he's going to hit, then he cuts through the fence but leaves a big gaping hole in it for us to find."

"Maybe he got spooked and made a run for it without taking time to disguise it," she said

"That's possible. Sure. But suppose it was planned that way. And another thing. Once inside, he tramps through the snow and goes all the way around one storage tank, then another, before going to the first of the really big ones and planting his explosives there. Why?"

Julie was about to comment, but I forestalled her.

"Maybe because he expects a tracking dog or two and he's still playing games with us. It's like he laid a trail of breadcrumbs for us to follow."

It was Julie's turn to say "Why?"

"We know he was watching us at Spruce Grove for sure. I'll bet he was watching us at some of the other places too. That means he knows what we look like, he knows we have tracking dogs and he knows what they look like, and he knows what our vehicles look like.... Do you remember the latest threat letter? It mentions a refinery, but not a specific one. I think this was set up so that no one else but us would think the threat was directed right here. Julie, I think he's after us or, more specifically me."

"Again, why?"

"I told you who I think it is, why I think he's so bitter, and why I think he has a grudge against the police right?"

"Right."

"Well, what I didn't tell you is that it was Silver and I that discovered his crime, Silver and I that tracked him down, and I'm the one that arrested him. That's why I think he's after me. Maybe Silver too."

"And this truck .... "

"This truck is so neither of us can be seen going anywhere near those two SUVs we parked on the side of the road."

While I drove, Julie radioed-in to request that the north-south road on the west side of the complex be barricaded from the southern end of the refinery to the railroad crossing that lay a few blocks beyond the northern end. When we had driven the refinery manager's truck away from the refinery site, I switched off its amber flashing lights and turned toward that same road. As I drove north on that road, I told Julie I was going to slow down as we passed our two parked SUVs so she could take a good look at them. As we passed them, she leaned out of her opened window and used her very bright flashlight to examine each.

"I'll be damned," she said, as she settled back into her seat and rolled her window back up.

"Well?"

"It's there all right. You have to look for it, but sitting on top of the front tire of the first SUV - your SUV - is a bright orange circle. About the same size as the one on the storage tank. If we'd walked back to get in the vehicles and begin the hunt, you'd have been coming at it from the ditch on the other side, which would have put you too close to the vehicle to have been able to see it. You'd have walked right by it and gotten in." I could hear the pain in her voice.

"It's OK Julie. Just one more trick of his that didn't work."

"So, now we go get him. Right?"

"Now we go get him. My guess is that he'll stay put for a while, watching for when we come back to the vehicles."

By this point, we'd come to the east-west road that lay just outside the northern edge of the refinery complex. I turned west and began looking for a good place to turn off the road and into the open field in which I thought Frank Smith would be holed-up, if he was in the area at all.

I had just turned off the road when my radio crackled to life.

"Echo Seven from Charlie, Frank, Mike," said one of the pilots.

"Echo Seven," I replied

"Nice beacon you've lit up for us. We may have spotted your suspect vehicle. There appears to be a black and white truck parked in the farmer's field due west of the refinery complex. It's approximately 120 metres west of the small storage tank in the extreme northwest and is exactly due west of the line of large storage tanks. Over."

"Thank you, Charlie, Frank, Mike. Are you able to take another pass while we attempt to locate the suspect?"

"Affirmative, Echo Seven, but be advised that visibility continues to drop. Estimate window for one more pass only and be warned that it's becoming more difficult to spot anything.

"Understood. We will have one team approach from the north and another from the south."

I drove into the field as far as I dared then stopped to let Julie and Scout get out. "If you spot him and are too close to risk speaking out loud, then give me three clicks with the mic, then a pause, then three more clicks. I'll drive around and come up from the south and do the same. Give me five minutes before you start."

"OK," she said, and hopped out.

"Julie!" I said, just before she closed the door. "Even though I think he's after me, in this falling snow you and Scout will look a lot like Silver and I."

"I know," she said, but her trademark smile was gone. Before I left, she gave Scout a good sniff of the blanket and groundsheet with Frank Smith's scent, then waved us off.

While Julie and Scout waited, I drove back to the road, then another hundred metres west before turning off the road once more and driving cross-country. Fortunately, it was a four-wheel drive truck so, although I had to go slowly, I had no trouble getting traction in the snow and dirt. When I estimated that I was well south of Frank's estimated position I turned left, drove for about a hundred metres, and stopped the truck. With any luck, I was due south of Julie and Scout, with Frank Smith somewhere in between us.

I gave Silver a good sniff of the recovered blanket and groundsheet, and sent him out to search. I would have liked to have been able to get one of the carbine rifles we had in the SUVs, but that couldn't be helped.

As Silver started out, my radio crackled.

"Echo Seven from Charlie, Frank, Mike," said one of the pilots.

"Echo Seven," I replied.

"We are passing over you now. We have both Members in sight. Subject vehicle is dead-centre between you. No sign of the subject. We are unable to make another pass." That meant that the worsening visibility was forcing them to return to the airport.

"Understand Charlie, Frank, Mike. Thank you. Echo Seven out."

It was just our two dog teams now, but at least we still had enough visibility to find our way. We were assisted in keeping our bearings, of course, by the massive fire that was burning in the storage tank. Glancing over, I could see that the fire department had arrived and were probably trying to figure out whether they could even put it out, or whether they would have to be content with containing it and letting it burn itself out without igniting anything else on the site.

It seemed like an eternity, but was probably only ten minutes, before my radio clicked three times, followed by Julie's voice.

"I can see the truck and will hold here until you find it too. No more voice communication. Please click once to acknowledge and three times when you arrive."

Good for you, I thought. Julie was playing it smart.

A few minutes later, I felt a tug on the leash and walked up to

Silver. Kneeling and placing a hand on his shoulder, I asked "Find something?"

Grrrr, said Silver. He had found the scent.

"OK. Good boy," I congratulated, in a low voice. "Quiet now," and I motioned him to advance.

Within five more metres I could see the outline of the truck. The top was covered by a thin layer of snow, but from the sides it looked exactly like the descriptions we'd been given. Flat black body with a white fibreglass top on the box.

On my radio I used the mic to give three clicks, a pause, then three clicks again.

I received a single click in reply. Message received.

I signalled Silver to continue searching. Frank Smith must have made several trips back and forth between his vantage point and his truck, because Silver was able to follow his trail easily. I got down on hands and knees and shortened the lead so that he and I were almost touching. He could tell from my body language and slow pace that we were hunting now, not just tracking.

It wasn't long before I could just make out a clump of low bushes ahead of us. Exactly the kind of place he would use for concealment, and when I stood fully upright for just a moment, I could see that it had a clear view of the northwest corner of the refinery area, with its intensely burning storage tank. With my hand on Silver's collar now, the two of us crept forward on our bellies.

Finally, I could just see the outline of a body ahead of me. Or, more accurately, a pair of boots sticking out of a lump that was covered with a sheet of some kind with lumps of snow on it. We had arrived.

Releasing his lead, I motioned for Silver to leave me and sweep out to one side and take up a flanking position. Long ago, he'd actually taught me this manoeuvre, and we'd done it so many times that it was almost instinctive between us. I was just shifting to ease my gun out of its holster when there was a muffled sound and the figure turned to look straight back at me.

"Hello Jim," I said "Time to set aside the gun."

"Damn," he said, before he turned back. In an instant, he took up his rifle again and I heard a shot, followed by another explosion some distance away. He'd detonated the explosives in my SUV.

"That's enough Jim. It's over. Set aside the gun."

He didn't, of course. What he did do was to get up with the rifle concealed from my sight along the length of his body, then turn and face me, with the rifle levelled at hip height - straight at me. We were so close to each other that I knew he could shoot me without shouldering the rifle.

I remained low, kneeling on the ground to give him the smallest possible target, with both arms bracing as I held my revolver aimed at his chest.

"I imagine that I was supposed to have been in the SUV when it went up?"

"Of course. How did you know?"

"Little things, really. My first clue was when we went looking for your observation point at the Spruce Grove pump station. When we found it, and your groundsheet and blanket, Silver began to growl in a way that suggested he recognized the scent and was unhappy about it That rarely happens, and I began to wonder who he could possibly know that might do what you were doing."

"That damn dog," he muttered.

"Yes. Then we found some security video that showed you from the back, and later we received some eyewitness descriptions of you from motels, restaurants, and even a coffee shop. Those gave us a rough description of you and your truck. They weren't enough by themselves, but a picture was beginning to take shape. Between the threat letters and everything else, it became obvious that someone was leading us around by the nose; we just didn't know who or why. Later, we discovered that you were travelling under the name Frank Smith and using stolen Ontario licence plates.

"The breakthrough for me came when I heard about your stopping to help that woman who ran out of gas coming east from Dawson Creek. The woman was so upset about how you'd cheated her that she complained to the gas station attendant and even imitated what you'd said to her. When the attendant tried to repeat her imitation, he told me you'd said something like 'Sure, but it'll cost you.' Now where had I heard that before? You used to say it to me and others in Radium City all the time. It even sounded a bit like you, the way he said it. That's when the lightbulb came on and I began to suspect it was you. When I made some enquiries, I learned that in August, convicted murderer James Dumont had escaped from custody while being treated at the Prince Albert hospital."

"I knew I should have left that woman there to freeze," he muttered.

"Probably, but you saw a chance to make a quick buck and couldn't resist it. Anyway, once I suspected you, things started to become a bit more clear. Rather than someone with a grudge against the police, it was someone with a grudge against me, personally. So, this whole ego trip of leading us around and planting bombs that you might or might not detonate was your way of regaining power over me, and the police, and the whole 'system' I suppose."

Jim just stood there in the falling snow, still pointing his rifle at me but not saying anything, so I continued.

"The thing here at the refinery was that it was clear we were being set-up for something. The way you lead us here, to this city, to this refinery. You even did a break-in here, which would have been foolish except that I bet you didn't even need the ammonium nitrate. You just wanted to make sure we'd be here so we'd know which refinery you were going to hit And you succeeded, Jim. You got us here and you pointed us at the target in a way that ensured that no one else would believe us. I bet you watched our every move as we wandered around trying to figure out why someone had broken in through the fence.

"So, tell me. If I'd gone up the stairs to look at the bomb, would you have detonated it right then?"

I didn't think he was going to answer at first, but then he said:

"No. I didn't think you'd actually find it.... How did you find it?"

"Silver, of course," I said surprised.

"That damn dog again! How did he know? After I put the package together, I washed it over and over again to remove any possible traces of the chemicals inside."

"Well, maybe you missed a very tiny bit. His nose is very sensitive and he can probably smell chemicals a million times better than we can[49]. I think the answer is much simpler though: I don't think he did smell the bomb chemicals; I think he smelled you."

"Me?"

"Yes. I told you that we found the blanket and groundsheet that you used when you were watching the Spruce Grove pump station two weeks ago. I kept it, and I gave both dogs a refresher sniff this morning. I think Silver smelled you on the bomb, and he remembered your scent. Anyway, you'd been so obvious about leading us here that I suspected you might try to end it all when you could get at just me, with my guard down, and having failed to prevent yet another explosion. So, I borrowed a truck and drove by the parked police vehicles. We saw the bomb on the front tire and just kept on driving."

"Damn dog," Jim muttered again. "I knew I should have shot him a long time ago, but I was afraid you'd give up or be replaced with another dog team.... Where is he anyway?"

"Oh, he's around somewhere, I imagine.... So what now Jim? Are you going to put the gun down?"

"You wish," he snarled. "I'm going to finish what I started. Right here. Right now. You Mounties never shoot first, so I can get in the first shot and I don't care whether you have a chance to shoot back. You've ruined my life anyway."

"She won't shoot first, but I will," came a woman's voice from off to one side. Out of the corner of my eye, I could see Julie crouched nearby with her revolver out and pointed at Jim in a solid, two-handed grip.

Jim had forgotten I had a partner and was so startled by the unexpected voice that he involuntarily turned to look in Julie's direction. As he did so, the rifle turned with him. When that happened, Julie and I gave a command to the dogs in unison, and from out of nowhere Silver and Scout popped up, one on each side of him. They had crept up unnoticed while I was talking to Jim and only needed a couple of bounds before they leapt into the air. Then each one grabbed an arm in their powerful jaws and clamped down hard, while their combined weight and momentum forced Jim to take a step back. Then, with a piercing shriek, he dropped to one knee with a dog resolutely hanging onto each forearm.

"Call them off," he shrieked again, in intense pain now.

"Drop the gun Jim," I said, as I stood up, while Julie moved in a few steps closer. Both of us with our guns pointed directly at him.

"Call them off. I'll kill all of you." He yelled again.

"But you won't, Jim. They'll tear your arms to shreds before they'll let you use that gun, and you'll just bleed to death here in the snow."

"Noooo," he said. His voice was beginning to falter now. While he stood there, panting and undecided, pain and shock made their way deeper into his body, then his muscles betrayed him, and the rifle fell to the ground.

As I went to retrieve the rifle we called off Scout and Silver, who immediately let go of Jim's arms and stepped back a few paces, but remained wary and watchful.

While Julie got onto her radio to call for help, I crouched down by Jim to begin first aid, starting with getting his coat off and cutting his shirt sleeves away. Both of his forearms were bleeding badly, and the many cuts were deep, but they weren't as bad as they would have been if Jim had continued to resist. Picking up the white sheet that Jim had used for camouflage, I used my knife to cut it into large pieces to use as compresses, and thin strips to use to tie them in place.

"Damn dogs," Jim gasped through the pain.

"A couple of Mounties' best friends," I agreed, continuing to bandage and tie. "Just stay sitting as you are. Help is on the way. Whether you want it or not."

"I knew you'd figure it all out," he said.... "You just did it too quickly.... Should have been at least one more day behind me.... Never should have seen the last bomb."

"I know," was all I said.

"Help is on the way," Julie reported. "If you'll give me the keys, I'll go get the refinery truck and bring it here. It's amber flashing lights will act like a beacon for the ambulance."

"Good thinking, Julie," I said, digging in a pocket for the keys.

"Thanks." Telling Scout to stay where he was, she went off.

"Tell me Jim," I asked while we waited, "was it really worth all this? All the damage and everything? One of the railway workers died in the Ontario explosion, you know."

"Fortunes of war," he gasped. "You ruined my life. I was going to be rich and retire young, and if it hadn't been for you and that damn dog, everything would have worked out as I planned. But instead, I got sent to that lousy prison."

"You murdered Norm!"

"Arrgh. Norm got in the way."

"Well, if you ever wanted to know when you lost my sympathy, it was when you murdered poor Norm."

I'm not sure whether he heard me. Jim had fainted.

Five minutes later, red and white flashing lights announced the arrival of an ambulance. It must have been called out to the refinery as a precaution, to have gotten to us so quickly.

Laurie Schramm

10 EPILOGUE

The last thing I had a chance to ask Jim was how he knew I would be called to the scene of the train derailment in Ontario back in November. He said that he'd read that there weren't many police dog service teams in any one region of the country, and even fewer with explosives training, so he'd figured there was a good chance I'd be called in. When I told him that it was only because the local OPP team was unavailable that Silver and I had been called, he shrugged and said that if not, he'd identified a secondary target closer to Ottawa to hit.

When I asked how he knew I was going to be at the Innisfail dog training centre two weeks later, he said that he'd learned about it by chance from a newspaper. He'd reached into his jacket and taken out a newspaper clipping, from the *Red Deer Advocate*, that contained an article about the Innisfail police dog service open house. Apparently, when the reporter heard about the planned dinner for the graduates and their families and me being the invited speaker, she got interested and tried digging up information on my old cases. All she'd found out about was Silver's and my explosives training, and my case in Radium City. The article even named Jim as the thief and murderer whom Silver and I had caught.

Great, I'd thought. *A chance newspaper article identifies me and inflames Jim.*

Beyond that, my involvement in the Radium City murder case was something for which my identity was never supposed to have become public knowledge, because by the time of the trial I'd been recruited into the Security Service for undercover work. Between that, and my involvement in several counterintelligence cases, my identity and job were becoming too well known by too many people, both in Canada and in foreign intelligence services.

It made me realize that my days in the Security Service, at least as a field operative, were becoming numbered.

Anyway, with Jim under guard in hospital and our reports typed-up and submitted, Julie and I had stayed one last night in Lloydminster. That gave Julie a chance to phone her parents and tell them about her successfully completed assignment, and me a chance to phone my fiancé Don, who was in Military Intelligence and based in Halifax. I'd been phoning Don about every second night since the beginning of the case and, even though we could only talk about innocuous things over an open phone line, it was always reassuring just to hear his voice. The down-side was having to tell him that we'd have to drive back to Edmonton to get my truck and, without an active police-case, I wouldn't be able to get Silver on a plane with me, so we weren't going to be able to get to Halifax to see him for Christmas like we'd hoped.

December 24, 1979
Edmonton, Alberta

On the day of Christmas eve, Julie and I took turns with the driving as we used the one surviving police SUV to get back to Edmonton. It was still snowing, so the nominally two-and-a-half to three-hour drive took us five hours, but it gave us time to chat and decompress, and we were at least able to avoid the fate of the several vehicles we spotted in the ditches beside the highway. These snow-covered and long abandoned vehicles had apparently succumbed to the late-night and/or early-morning ice on the roads, whereas we had purposely waited for the morning snowplows and sanders to do their work before venturing out ourselves.

We were just approaching the outskirts of the city when the police radio came to life. Since Julie was driving at the time, I reached for the mic to acknowledge the call.

"Proceed to CFB Edmonton to receive a package from AIRCOM."

Having been there before, I knew that Canadian Forces Base

Edmonton was just north of Edmonton, and that it is often still referred to as Namao, one of the base's earlier names, by the locals and even many of the serving military. Having a military fiancé, and having served on numerous assignments involving the Canadian Forces, I also knew that AIRCOM was military language for Air Command[50].

"What's all that about?" asked Julie, after I had acknowledged and signed off the radio.

"No idea," I said. "Maybe the air force is delivering Christmas presents for Santa Claus this year."

We both chuckled, but I really had no idea what it could be, unless my bosses in Ottawa had another assignment for me already.

Not on Christmas Eve! I thought to myself, but I knew better, and I'd become used to late-night phone calls that ripped me out of bed and had Silver and I rushing off to one part of the country or another.

When we reached the main security gate at the airbase, we had to stop and identify ourselves. "Corporal Alexandra Houston, Constable Julie Sawyer, and two police dogs," the Sergeant in charge of the gate detail read off from a clipboard, having checked our IDs. He waved us to one of the hangers and said someone would meet us there. So, Julie switched on our flashing, emergency lights and drove us to the designated hanger.

There waiting for us was a fully armed military police sergeant, and I had a sudden suspicion he might be from the intelligence side of the organization. The sergeant didn't offer us any clues however, he simply checked our IDs, showed us a place to park, and then led us to a spartan waiting room in the hangar.

There was coffee available, so we served ourselves and settled down to wait. For the next half hour absolutely nothing happened, and Julie and I and the dogs were becoming restless when the same sergeant came back to announce that the aircraft with our package was on final approach and expected to land soon.

With nothing better to do, Julie and I got up to stand by the hanger entrance and watch to see what kind of aircraft it was. Julie bet it would be a helicopter, while I predicted it would be a Hercules[51].

We discovered how wrong we were when we almost collapsed under the stunning roar as a Voodoo fighter jet[52] made a low-level pass right over our heads then screamed past and beyond. As we watched, it made a tight banking turn and then glided smoothly onto one of the runways.

As the jet taxied towards us after landing, the long canopy was raised to reveal two helmeted heads. After the jet had been waved into position in front of the hanger, the pilot climbed out from the front seat and down a short ladder to the ground, followed by the person in the back. It wasn't until he reached the ground and removed his flying helmet that I realized it was Don, but by that time my body was already running.

I can run pretty fast in a short sprint, but not as fast as Silver can. Before I could reach Don, Silver had sprinted past me and thrown himself at Don so that they collided chest to chest and were both knocked to the ground. By the time I reached them Silver had licked every bit of Don's skin that he could find before I was able to call him off, help Don up and collapse into his arms.

"You're the package?" I asked, hopefully.

"I'm the package," he confirmed. "Your Assistant Commissioner called my Admiral, and the two of them conspired to give us both the same Christmas present: Christmas Day, Boxing Day and three days leave together.

"'After that, the two of you get your butts back to work where you belong,' the Admiral told me, with that scowl he does so well, and in his best crusty-curmudgeon voice. But I could see in his eyes what he really meant."

"And the jet?"

"Dead-heading. I got a lift on a Hercules that was going to CFB Trenton, and from there on the Voodoo that was coming here anyway, on its way to CFB Cold Lake. The second seat was going to be empty, so no extra cost to the taxpayers."

So, I got the best Christmas presents ever. A successfully completed mission, which Silver and I managed to survive, and a chance to be with my fiancé for Christmas.

Julie accepted our invitation to spent it with us, on behalf of herself and Scout, and it was... wonderful!

□ □ □

... Alex and Silver will return.

Laurie Schramm

SUMMARY

When RCMP Corporal Alexandra Houston and her police-service-dog partner Silver are called to the scene of a train derailment in Central Canada, the horror of the devastation is magnified by their discovery that it was intentionally caused; and by a bomb. The bombing turns out to be the first of many, leading Alex and Silver across Western Canada as they try to figure out where the next strikes will occur - and how to stop them.

Laurie Schramm

ABOUT THE AUTHOR

Laurie Schramm comes from an RCMP family, grew up while living in the RCMP Barracks (Depot Division) in Regina, Saskatchewan, and spent several summers working as a civilian for the RCMP while in high school and university. Early personal influences included not only the real-life RCMP culture but also Hollywood's versions via such classics as *Rose Marie*, and *Susannah of the Mounties*. Many of the events described in this novel are based on the author's real life, although not necessarily within an RCMP context.

For more information, see Laurier L. Schramm on **Linked** in

and:

www.laurieschramm.ca

Laurie Schramm

ENDNOTES

1. Prince Albert's Holy Family Hospital closed in 1997.
2. $200 in 1979 would be worth about C$790 in 2023.
3. The Province of Alberta didn't switch their motor vehicle licensing requirement from two plates to one (at the rear) until 1992.
4. This was an illusion on his part. The manufacture of explosives is federally regulated in Canada and requires a permit.
5. I have left out some of the specific component names, and all of the quantities and particle sizes, in order to avoid providing a recipe for use in real life.
6. This account is entirely fictional but, in real life, a binary exploding target package of the kind described here would eventually be developed in 1996, subsequently patented, and marketed as small, exploding targets for use in target practice, training, and shooting competitions, under the trade-name Tannerite® Binary Exploding Rifle Targets. See: D.J. Tanner, "Binary Exploding Target, Package, Process and Product," U.S. Patent 6,848,366 B1, Feb. 1, 2005.
7. In later years, beginning in 1988, cabooses were phased out of Canadian railways. Since then, trains have been operated by an engineer and a conductor, both of whom ride in the locomotive.
8. In real life, CP Train 54 with three locomotives and 106 cars accidentally derailed as it was passing through Mississauga,

Ontario on November 10, 1979. It was carrying a tanker of chlorine and 39 tankers filled with a variety of flammable materials, including propane and butane. Some of the latter went up in flames, causing huge fireballs and concerns that the chlorine might get converted to deadly phosgene ('Mustard Gas'). As a result, the entire region, comprising some 250,000 people, was evacuated – the largest evacuation in North American history. See for example: Heritage Mississauga, "Mississauga Train Derailment," Mississauga Heritage Foundation, Mississauga, ON, 2018, https://heritagemississauga.com/mississauga-train-derailment/

9. Ontario Provincial Police.

10. A tributary of the Ottawa River. No connection to the U.S. river of the same name.

11. This was relatively new. In 1976, the Ottawa Police Service added a group of specially-trained members to its Tactical Unit to better prepare it to deal with domestic and terrorist bomb threats. This sub-unit was colloquially known as the 'Bomb Squad.'

12. Currently named Forensic Science and Identification Services (FS&IS).

13. In real-life, it was an RCMP Chaplain who taught me how to 'properly' shake hands. When someone extends their hand towards you, move quickly to ensure that your hands lock all the way up to the base of the vee between your thumb and forefinger. "Do it this way," he said as he demonstrated the grip, "and you'll never get your fingers crushed. Take the word of someone that has survived many thousands of handshakes outside the front doors of churches and chapels."

14. The city of Ottawa houses two of Canada's 'Top 20' universities: Carleton University and the University of Ottawa.

15. The RCMP's Police Dog Service (PDS) Training Centre is located near Innisfail, Alberta.

16. See P. Barnett, "Requests About Explosives and Illicit Drugs: A New Paradigm," *The Reference Librarian*, Vol. 55, No. 2, 2014, pp. 118-127.

17. Part of the Explosives Regulatory Division within Natural Resources Canada.

18. The gas chromatograph coupled with a mass spectrometer (GC-MS) has been referred to as "chemist's gold," meaning the

gold standard for the forensic analysis of unknown substances in a sample. Gas chromatography is used to separate the different kinds of molecules in a mixture, and then mass spectrometry is used to identify and quantify each type of separated molecules.

19. See *An Inconspicuous Mountie* (Amazon, Seattle, WA, 2019, ISBN: 978-1-9994940-2-5).

20. See *An Inconvenient Mountie* (Amazon, Seattle, WA, 2018, ISBN: 978-1-9994940-0-1).

21. See *An International Mountie* (Amazon, Seattle, WA, 2020, ISBN: 978-1-9994940-6-3).

22. North American Air Defense Command (at the time of this story); now termed North American Aerospace Defense Command. NORAD is a joint U.S.-Canada operation providing aerospace warning and protection for Canada and the continental U.S.

23. L.M. Montgomery, *Anne of Green Gables*, originally published by L.C. Page, Boston, MA, in 1908.

24. Chinook winds originate from moist air moving inland from the Pacific Ocean and up the western slopes of the Rocky Mountains. As the moist air rises, it expands, cools, and loses its moisture in the form of rain and snow as it traverses the mountain tops. On the eastern side of the mountains, the dry air warms-up as it loses altitude and sweeps onto the prairies of southern Alberta. In Alberta, these are called Chinook winds, in other parts of the world, similar winds are called *Föhn* winds. A Chinook wind can temporarily raise the surface temperature in southern Alberta by as much as 20 °C (or more).

25. The approximate outdoor evacuation distance for a 'typical' pipe bomb.

26. The Trans Mountain Pipeline was built between 1952 and 1953 to transport crude and refined oil from Edmonton, Alberta to Burnaby, British Columbia. The Trans Mountain Pipeline Company was originally owned by Canadian Bechtel Ltd. and Standard Oil, later by Kinder Morgan, and since 2018 by the Government of Canada.

27. See references 19, 20, and 21 above, plus: *An Indestructible Mountie* (ISBN: 978-1-9994940-4-9), *An Inseparable Mountie*

(ISBN: 978-1-7772424-0-4), *An Indispensable Mountie* (ISBN: 978-1-7772424-2-8), *An Inexorable Mountie* (ISBN: 978-1-7772424-4-2), and *An Intrepid Mountie* (ISBN: 978-1-7772424-6-6).

28. Azrael is an archangel of death and retribution in some theologies. The Arabic name is *Izrāīl*.

29. The Canadian Police Information Centre (CPIC) is Canada's national police database. When the author worked at CPIC in 1971 (before its launch), we referred to it by spelling out the acronym's letters – 'C-P-I-C' - but after the system became operational in 1972, people in the field began to refer to it as 'seapick.' See: B. Sharp, "*Cop*," Friesen Press, Victoria, BC, 2014.

30. At the time of writing, the Trans-Mountain Pipeline is undergoing a major expansion that is expected to add approximately 980 kilometres of parallel pipeline, new pump stations and terminals, and a new dock complex. The descriptions in this book all refer to the original pipeline that was built in the early 1950s and still in use to the present day.

31. The pressure in a long-distance pipeline drops as its contents move farther away from the discharge point of one pump station and towards the suction-end of the next pump station. The pump stations boost the pressure back up, and are located at various points that are determined by the local terrain and pipeline diameter.

32. The RCMP established its Air Service (now Air Services Directorate) in 1937, beginning with four de Havilland Dragonfly aircraft. At the time of this story (1979/80), the Force had 27 aircraft posted at 23 locations across Canada. For an introduction to the history of RCMP aircraft usage, see: RCMP Media Relations, "Royal Canadian Mounted Police Air Services: 1937-2007 - 70 years of Service to the RCMP and Citizens of Canada," Government of Canada, 31 May 2007, https://www.canada.ca/en/news/archive/2007/05/royal-canadian-mounted-police-air-services-1937-2007-70-years-service-rcmp-citizens-canada.html

33. Photographs taken at a low angle relative to the earth's surface are referrer to as low-oblique photographs.

34. Whiteboards began to increase in popularity after practical dry-erase markers for them became available in the late 1970s. At

the time of this story, they would have been viewed as a leading-edge innovation.

35. Nepean, Ontario had its own police force until it was amalgamated into the Ottawa-Carleton Regional Police Service in 1995 (since renamed Ottawa Police Service).

36. See *An International Mountie* (Amazon, Seattle, WA, 2020, ISBN: 978-1-9994940-6-3).

37. In 1979, Canadian-vehicle licence plate colours were as follows: BC: white on medium blue, AB: black on yellow, SK: green on white, MB: purple on yellow, ON: blue on white, QC: blue on white, NB: green on white, NS: blue on white, PEI: white on black, NF: blue on orange, YK: red on white, and NWT: turquoise on white (polar bear shape). The territory of Nunavut wasn't formed until April, 1999.

38. Identification Services. A branch of the RCMP providing, among other things, a national repository for fingerprint records. A computer system for automated fingerprint classification, storage and retrieval was launched in 1970, but it took a dozen years to fully digitize and integrate the criminal fingerprint files.

39. By the end of the 1970s, fax machines had become standard business equipment in North America.

40. See: British Columbia. Legislative Assembly, "Minister of Energy, Mines and Petroleum Resources Annual Report 1979," Government Printer, Victoria, BC, 1983.

41. See: Canada, "Canada Year Book 1978-79," Statistics Canada, Ottawa, 1979.

42. Nalgene is a registered trademark. At the time of this story, it was owned by Nalge Company, which later became a subsidiary of Fisher Scientific, now Thermo Fisher Scientific.

43. The 'Christmas tree' on an oil or gas well is the arrangement of pipes and other equipment that rises vertically above-ground at the wellhead. It includes the pipe through which the oil and/or gas flows, plus a number of valves, gauges, by-passes, and flow-controllers so that the flow can be controlled and adjusted. The name comes from imagining the whole assembly as being something like a Christmas tree, with all its decorations.

44. One Imperial gallon is approximately 4.55 litres. In 1979, the average retail price of gasoline in the Prairie provinces was

about $0.22 per litre, so one Imperial gallon would have cost about one dollar.

45. The 1976 census lists the Lloydminster population at 10,311, including the residents on each side of the provincial border.

46. At the time of this story there were approximately 39 refineries operating in Canada, with at least one located in almost every province. By the time of writing, 23 of these refineries had been closed and two new ones commissioned, for a total of 18 (not including the Husky heavy-oil upgrader).

47. "'Will you walk into my parlour?' said the Spider to the Fly" is the first line of *The Spider and the Fly*, a poem by Mary Howitt; published in 1829.

48. C-FMPN was a de Havilland Canada Inc., DHC-6 Twin Otter Series 300 aircraft. Originally registered CF-MPN, it was delivered to RCMP Air Services in 1971 and based in Edmonton. It was sold to the private sector in 1999, where it changed owners (and countries) several times, and was still reported to be in service at the time of writing. Reference: TwinOtterArchive.com, Dec. 2022.

49. On the sensitivity of an explosives-trained dog, a 2002 Sandia National Laboratories (U.S.) report commented, in part, that: "The vapor sensing capabilities of dogs are almost universally undisputed; however, measuring the dogs' performance at ultratrace vapor levels is difficult because the sensitivity of chemical measurement technology is far inferior compared to that of the dog." In fact, there is some evidence that some dogs are capable of sensing as little as a single molecule per sniff (that's 10^{-10} parts-per trillion!). See: J.M. Phelan and S.W. Webb, "Chemical Sensing for Buried Landmines - Fundamental Processes Influencing Trace Chemical Detection," Sandia National Laboratories, Albuquerque, NM, Report SAND2002-0909, May, 2002.

50. The Canadian Air Force originated with two-squadrons that fought in the First World War. In 1924, an expanded version became the Royal Canadian Air Force (RCAF). By the end of the Second World War, the RCAF had grown again, and was one of the largest of the allied air forces. All of Canada's armed forces were combined into a single body in 1968, under the government's unification policy of the time, with specific air force groups assigned to specific commands. In 1975, the

aviation components were essentially reunited under Air Command (AIRCOM) until 2011, at which time AIRCOM was changed back to its earlier name: Royal Canadian Air Force (RCAF).

51. The RCAF's C-130H Hercules are four-engine-turboprop, tactical-transport aircraft. Designed to operate from low quality, short airstrips, they have been used for everything from troop and equipment transport, to search and rescue, and even air-to-air refueling operations.

52. The McDonnell CF-101B Voodoo was a supersonic, all-weather-interceptor jet fighter. They were a variant of the U.S. F101 aircraft. The 'B' designation referred to the dual-seat version.

Laurie Schramm

ADVENTURES OF THE FIRST WOMAN MOUNTIE

Individual Novels	Collections
Bk 1: *An Inconvenient Mountie*	
Bk 2: *An Inconspicuous Mountie*	*Adventures of the First Woman Mountie.*
Bk 3: *An Indestructible Mountie*	*Omnibus Volume 1*
Bk 4: *An International Mountie*	
Bk 5: *An Inseparable Mountie*	
Bk 6: *An Indispensable Mountie*	*Adventures of the First Woman Mountie II:*
Bk 7: *An Inexorable Mountie*	*The Second Omnibus*
Bk 8: *An Intrepid Mountie*	
Bk 9: *An Intimate Mountie*	
Bk 10: *An Ineradicable Mountie*	*Adventures of the First Woman Mountie III:*
Bk 11: *An Incommunicado Mountie*	*The Third Omnibus (Forthcoming)*
Bk 12: *An Instructive Mountie*	

www.laurieschramm.ca

SUMMARIES

An Inconvenient Mountie (Book 1). 1975. Alexandra Houston is asked to join RCMP as its first woman Member - as a pilot project. She accepts, hoping it will fulfil her dream of doing "some real policing," while not realizing that she should be careful what she asks for. Her first posting is to a remote part of Northern Saskatchewan, where no one is used to dealing with a female Mountie and her adventures in small-town policing are compounded by crises, crime, and mystery.

An Inconspicuous Mountie (Book 2). 1976. Alex and her dog Silver are training to work as an undercover team. Meanwhile, trouble is brewing north of Fort McMurray, Alberta where not everyone is happy with the development of the massive oil sands mines and tensions are running high. Before their training is complete, a pipeline is bombed, and new threats emerge. As Alex and Silver are sent in, this time they need to be … inconspicuous.

An Indestructible Mountie (Book 3). 1977. A hiker on Cape Breton Island discovers a strange installation hidden in the forest, on an oceanside cliff. Word of her discovery reaches the RCMP Security Service, where it sets off alarm bells, and Alex and Silver are sent in. As they investigate, a technological curiosity from the Second World War turns out to be the centre-piece of something current, and sinister. This time Alex and Silver will need to be… indestructible.

An International Mountie (Book 4). Alex finally gets a break from a series of hair-raising assignments and heads for Alaska on vacation. While there she hopes to investigate Silver's origins and hike the famous Chilkoot Trail. Meanwhile, a young Girl Guide gets lost in the wilds of Alaska and experiences, first-hand, the meaning of the Guides and Scouts motto: "*Be Prepared.*"

An Inseparable Mountie (**Book 5**). Called away from vacation in Alaska, Alex and Silver are inserted into an unfolding mystery in northwest British Columbia. Second World War artillery shells seem to be washing up on a beach and having disturbing effects on the kids that find them. These catch the attention of Military Intelligence as well, and Canadian Forces Lieutenant Don Harrison joins them in a search that will take them into danger once more.

An Indispensable Mountie (**Book 6**). 1978. When a Soviet nuclear-powered spy satellite veers off course and explodes over Canada's north, a military search operation is launched to recover the radioactive pieces. But there is a search within the search, as Alex and Silver are sent in undercover to discover whether one of the satellite's top-secret components may have survived. As they search a virtually uninhabited wasteland, they soon discover that aircraft malfunctions and the Arctic cold are the least of their problems.

An Inexorable Mountie (**Book 7**). Alex boards a cross-Canada train to look for security vulnerabilities in advance of an upcoming VIP trip. At least, that's her cover assignment. In reality, Alex and Silver are after bigger game. As they roll through the Atlantic Provinces, Central Canada, and the Prairies, Alex notices some strange behaviours on the part of several of her fellow passengers. These evolve into break-ins, intrigue, and a growing certainty that quite a few people on the train besides herself are not who they seem to be.

An Intrepid Mountie (**Book 8**). When Alex and Silver experience a chance encounter with two suspicious characters on the front lawn of Canada's Parliament Buildings, Alex decides to do a little digging. The results take them from the Pacific coast of British Columbia to the Atlantic coasts of Newfoundland and Labrador, on the trail of a professional agitator whose appearances at organized protest events seem to coincide with a trail of violence, injuries, and death.

An Intimate Mountie (**Book 9**). No sooner does Alex get engaged than she and her fiancé are invited to a family funeral and reunion at a lodge on Cape Breton Island. There, Alex learns about an ancient family curse, experiences suspicious events, and hears about still others from family members. Following a near-death experience, she begins investigating in earnest. When one of the lodge staff is found murdered, she has to move quickly if she is to figure out what's been going on and identify the killer before another murder takes place.

An Ineradicable Mountie (**Book 10**). 1979. When a young American woman experiences two attempted kidnappings in two successive days, Alex and Silver are assigned to protect her from some surprisingly persistent and well-informed pursuers while the woman's father concludes secret international negotiations. To buy time, they hide out in a secret, underground military installation, but their location is soon discovered and they find themselves under siege. With stealth and secrecy gone Alex realizes that, this time, she may have to shoot her way out of trouble.

An Incommunicado Mountie (**Book 11**). Alex, her fiancé Don, and Silver make a late-fall visit to a brand-new ski lodge high up in the Canadian Rockies. After only a short period of hiking and mountaineering in this idyllic setting, their vacation is threatened by a snow-storm that cuts off both power and access to the lodge. While they and a group of university students wait out the storm, a suspicious death puts Alex on the trail of a murderer.

An Instructive Mountie (**Book 12**). When Alex and Silver are called to the scene of a train derailment in Central Canada, the horror of the devastation is magnified by their discovery that it was intentionally caused; and by a bomb. The bombing turns out to be the first of many, leading Alex and Silver across Western Canada as they try to figure out where the next strikes will occur - and how to stop them.

Adventures of the First
Woman Mountie

Laurie Schramm